Eli B. Toresen

Dangerous Summer

Part 1:
The Arsonist

Copyright: Text © 2005 by Eli B. Toresen
Published by Pony, Stabenfeldt A/S
Cover photos: Fotograf Kallen, Elin M. Ellingsen
Cover layout: Stabenfeldt A/S
Translated by Osa K. Bondhus
Edited by Bobbie Chase
Printed in Germany 2005

ISBN 82-591-1166-7

Chapter 1

"Finally, summer vacation! No homework, and no more boring classes for over two months!" I hollered in pure joy as I ran from the school bus and up our driveway. Before entering the house, I stopped for a moment, as I always did, and looked over toward the closest horse pasture. I could see Grenada, one of our breeding mares, along with her filly foal, Niobe. Even though I was used to this sight, I never got tired of admiring our beautiful Arabian horses.

"You're so lucky, Eva, having parents who run a stud farm! "my best friend Sarah often says. "Imagine being able to be around horses all day long! I wish my parents were interested in horses."

Yes, of course I knew I was lucky. Sarah's mom can't stand horses, so every time Sarah comes home after having been in our stables, her mom pretty much has an anxiety attack from that "horrible horse stench," and demands that Sarah disinfect both herself and her clothes before she gets into the house. It's unbelievable how stupid some grown-ups can be.

The only bad thing right now was that Sarah wasn't going to be home this summer. I had been looking forward to us taking rides together and having loads of fun, but then her parents suddenly decided that their whole family would go to the Caribbean for something they called island hopping. They would be gone for a whole month, maybe longer. Which meant that all my plans went down the drain! Oh well, I told myself. I can manage to make this a fun summer anyway. Who could possibly get bored on a farm full of horses?

Niobe jumped around happily out in the pasture, and I couldn't help smiling. She was so cute! It was incredible that she managed to keep those long, wobbly legs under control. It looked almost as if they had a life of their own.

I thought about my own fullblood Arabian horse, Aron, who was born in the spring five years ago. He had been very little and frail, with big, brown eyes that sort of looked like they were asking for help. I fell instantly for that helpless creature, and had begged my mom and dad relentlessly to let me have him and to not sell him. My dad had been reluctant in the beginning, because he felt that I ought to have one of the bigger and stronger foals, and preferably a filly foal, if I were to have my own horse. He was worried that Aron would be trouble. But I persisted, and he eventually gave in on the condition that Aron be castrated. Dad refused to take the risk of having me ride a boisterous stallion. And of course I agreed. I would have agreed to anything just to get Aron, and I have never regretted my choice for a moment. Before we knew it, Aron had grown into a big strong horse. And with his reddish brown coloring, three white socks and a white blaze stretching all the way from the mane down to the muzzle, he was, in my opinion, the most beautiful horse in the world.

The thought of actually owning this fantastic horse always makes me warm with happiness inside, and while I hurried into the house, I was already planning some long, fun rides for him and me. This was going to be a great summer vacation, no matter what!

"What?! Are you telling me Anna is coming here tomorrow to stay for a whole month?" I stared at my mom in disbelief. My good mood was gone in a flash. "But why? She can't stand us!"

My mom's face got an irritated expression. "Honestly, Eva, what a thing to say!" she exclaimed. "Anna doesn't have anything against us. Why should she? The two of you had a perfectly good time together last time Anna and her parents were here for a visit."

"Good time?" I shook my head. Was my mom having a lapse of memory? "Anna was scared of everything, and would barely even go outside the house!" I said angrily. "She wouldn't go to the stable, because there were horses, and they were big and dangerous.

6

Nor would she go anywhere in the woods or in the fields, because a horse might show up there, too, or maybe a fierce dog!" I looked at her pleadingly. "Really, Mom! Anna will have a lousy time here. And what about me? Am I supposed to not ride for a whole month, and just sit inside playing board games with that wimp? No way!"

Mom sat down at the kitchen table and motioned for me to sit down too. Reluctantly I dropped down on a chair, while all kinds of depressing thoughts whirled through my mind. I saw my summer vacation plans once more going down the drain.

"Nobody is going to demand that you sit inside and play board games," said my mom, half in irritation and half in laughter. "Remember, it's been two years since Anna was here last. I'm sure she has changed quite a bit over those two years, and I doubt she'll still be scared of dogs and horses. Most people outgrow those kinds of fears."

"Then why are so many grown-ups scared of dogs?" I objected skeptically. "If what you're saying is true, I mean, that they outgrow their fears."

My mom didn't answer that. "I just think you should give Anna a chance," was all she said. "Besides, this is not really up for discussion. What kind of person would I be if I told my own sister that her daughter is not welcome here while they're away? You know how sick Aunt Joanne has been this last year, right?"

I nodded. Anna's mom had gotten a rare viral disease that had forced her to stay in bed for months until she finally recovered.

"And now they've been lucky enough to win a trip for two, flying around the globe, with hotels and everything paid for. The least we can do is be there for them now and take Anna while they're gone."

"But why can't she stay home with her brothers?" I said in a final attempt to avoid this very unappealing visit. Anna's brothers were 18 and 20 years old, so why couldn't she just stay with them?

"Because neither of them will be home this summer," said my mom. "Their band has been offered a summer job on a cruise ship,

7

so they'll be gone the entire summer. Please Eva, work with me here," she pleaded. "Give Anna a chance! You two are the same age, and I'm sure you can find some fun things to do together. Who knows? This could be the most exciting summer vacation you've ever had."

I didn't know then how right my mom would be on that particular point, though not exactly in the way she meant.

Later, when I was standing outside the stable grooming Aron, I was still upset by the thought of Anna coming. The last time I had seen her, she was this delicate little thing, with a high, whiny voice that had irritated me immensely. I hoped, for both our sakes, that she really had changed since then. I would know soon enough. My mom was going to pick her up at the airport around four o-clock the next day, which meant I barely had 24 hours to enjoy my freedom before she showed up.

"We'll have to make the most of the time we have," I sighed, scratching Aron's forehead. He rubbed his head contentedly against my arm and gave a low neigh. Then he started sniffing my pockets, as if expecting a treat to somehow miraculously appear there.

"Stop that, you greedy boy," I said laughingly. "You've already had both an apple and a carrot. That should do." Aron shook his head, making his mane flap. He apparently thought he deserved more.

I put the saddle on and tightened it well. Then I waited a little, and tightened it one more time. That's because Aron tends to fill his belly with air when I'm tightening the cinch. In the past he had frequently tricked me, which meant that the saddle would slip around after I got up on his back. By now I knew all of his tricks, so he couldn't fool me anymore.

While I was working on the saddle, my dad came bouncing by in our pickup truck. He stopped the truck and stuck his head out the open window. "Some people sure have a good life," he said with an exaggerated sigh. "But you go right ahead and enjoy your fun ride. Don't think about your poor old dad slaving away from dusk 'til dawn!"

I looked at him in astonishment, thinking for a moment that he was serious. But then I saw the teasing look in his eyes.

"And what's breaking your back, you poor old man?" I teased right back. "Is it too much for you to sit behind that wheel?"

"Cheeky!" laughed Dad. "I'm off to take down the remaining roof pans on the Hansen house, to make everything ready for the demolition crew."

"I thought they weren't coming for another two weeks," I replied. "What's the rush?"

"Oh, it's good to get it out of the way," said Dad. "Then I won't have to worry about it anymore."

I nodded. It had only been a few weeks since we took over the Hansen ranch. The ranch had been sold at a forced auction, after the owner, Randall Hansen, had been declared bankrupt.

He had neglected his animals for a long time, and finally lost the right to keep any. Apparently he had neglected his bills as well, because he owed money left and right. He ended up losing the whole ranch, and my parents had bought it at auction for a very reasonable price. We planned to use the additional property for growing hay and other feed for our horses.

The house on the ranch, however, was in such bad shape that it had to be torn down. The barn had already been removed. I was glad about that. I wouldn't have wanted any of our horses to live in a place where so many animals had suffered for so long. Just the thought of it made me shudder.

It was unbelievable to me how anyone could treat animals that way, and what made it worse was that it took so long before the abuse had been discovered, because Randall Hansen had been a loner who didn't socialize with other people in town.

Dad had told me that Mr. Hansen showed up at the auction and badmouthed everyone who bid on his property. The sheriff finally had to remove him by force. Fortunately by now he had left town, having stowed his belongings into an old camper and taken off. I doubted there was anyone who would miss him.

I was just about to ride out of the farmyard when Mom showed up. "Good news," she shouted.

Yes! I thought. Anna isn't coming after all. But it wasn't about Anna.

"It will be quite an invasion of cousins around here this summer," laughed my mom. "Rachel just called and asked if we need any help at the stable this summer. I said yes, of course. I assume you don't have any objections?"

"Oh, that's great!" I screamed with delight. "My vacation is saved!"

My cousin Rachel is 17, and four years older than Anna and I, but despite the age difference she has never treated me like a little kid. Rachel is really nice, and a very good rider. We have been together quite a bit, because Rachel lives only two hours away.

"When is she coming?" I asked excitedly. "We have to make room for Nùpur in the stable and find out which pasture he should be in."

Nùpur is Rachel's Icelandic horse. He's very cute, with golden brown coloring and a thick mane and tail. Of course I think Aron is prettier, but all horse owners probably think that way about their own horses. If I couldn't have an Arabian, however, I would most likely choose an Icelandic horse. They're tough and hardy, just like the Arabians, but with a good temper. They can also be stubborn and rowdy, which is certainly true for Arabians as well.

"She's coming tonight, but she won't be bringing Nùpur," said Mom. "He's been injured."

"Oh, no!" I said, horrified. "Is it serious?"

"No, no, just a minor injury in the right hind leg. He'll be as good as new again," said my mom reassuringly. "But Rachel won't be able to ride him for about a month, so he'll stay in a pasture with some other horses over the summer."

"I can't believe Rachel wants to leave him," I said, somewhat puzzled, while stroking Aron's neck. He was starting to get impatient. Weren't we supposed to go for a ride? he seemed to ask. Then why are we just standing around in the farmyard? He stomped his forelegs and snorted loudly.

10

"I talked to her mother briefly," said Mom. "Seems it had something to do with a boy. Some problem that has made Rachel want to get away for a while."

I nodded as I started thinking that maybe some boyfriend had broken up with her. If Rachel was sad because of a boy she liked, she might certainly feel the need to disappear for a few weeks.

I rode down the gravel road leading from our farm to the woods while I thought about how much fun it would be to have Rachel around for a whole month. Even if she were supposed to work at the stud, we would have plenty of time to go for rides together, if we didn't have to sit at home and take care of wimpy little Anna, that is! No, I was not going to let the thought of Anna ruin my mood again.

I stretched forward in the saddle and patted Aron's neck. He flapped his ears and bent his neck, which was a sure sign that he was happy and content. I was looking forward to getting onto the nice trail in the woods, where I could take him into a gallop. Unfortunately, I had to follow the marked public trail first. No matter how slowly and carefully I rode there, I almost always got some more or less crabby comment from a hiker or runner who thought horses should be forbidden on the trails. I think that is so unfair, especially coming from runners. They are hardly the ones to complain, since they usually run in groups of ten to twelve people, and are certainly not showing much consideration for hikers. They fill the whole trail, and seem to think they own it. It's up to the other people who happen to be on the trail to scramble out of the way as best they can. I have never seen any horseback rider who behaved like that, so why some people get so upset by the sight of a horse is beyond me.

This time, however, I managed to get to the unmarked forest trails without meeting a single grumpy runner or irritable senior. It was wonderful to feel Aron really stretch out beneath me as he went into a thundering gallop. I knew that my mom and dad wouldn't have liked that I galloped in the woods by myself, but right here the trail was so straight and flat that it couldn't possibly be dangerous. No sooner had I thought so than a black and white

11

lightning bolt shot out of the bushes and flew straight into Aron's legs. The horse stopped so fast I almost got thrown out of the saddle. Luckily I managed to hold on.

"Boris!" I screamed, while my heart beat so hard from the shock that I could feel it all the way up in my throat. "What are you doing here? Are you aware of how close you came to causing a serious accident?"

The black and white dog didn't look very guilty. He just scuttled about around Aron's legs, barking excitedly. Aron started stomping irritably with his forelegs, while he squinted angrily at the annoying furball who had ruined his gallop.

I got out of the saddle and picked Boris up. My legs were still shaking under me, because I was very much aware of how badly this could have ended if Aron had stumbled and fallen instead of just coming to an abrupt stop.

"Bad dog," I said sternly, and got my face licked by an excited dog with a slobbery tongue in return. I couldn't help smiling. Boris is simply one of a kind, but sometimes he can create some very dangerous situations. He lives on one of the neighboring farms, but the elderly couple that own him are getting so frail that they can't really control him anymore. Hence Boris is a frequent guest over at our stud farm, where he is getting all the attention he needs. He is actually the world's cutest and sweetest little dog, but he has the unfortunate habit of playing around with the horses and running in between their legs whenever he gets a chance. The horses aren't the slightest bit afraid of him, but they sometimes get so annoyed with him that they make a counter attack. It's a miracle that Boris hasn't been seriously injured. He has been kicked by an agitated horse more than once, and come away from it without any lasting damage every time. My dad has on occasion threatened to send that bothersome dog off to the slaughterhouse, but he doesn't mean it. None of us is a bigger sucker for Boris's cute little wagging tail and persuasive brown eyes than he is.

What I didn't understand at that moment was what Boris was doing there, so far from home. Usually he stays home or keeps to our farm. Was it possible that he had followed us without my noticing? Yeah, I guess that wasn't too unbelievable. Boris was in fact a very intelligent dog. I held him in front of me in the saddle while I rode back home at a walking pace. At first Aron was throwing suspicious glances back at us, checking to see what was going on up there on his back, but he eventually relaxed and accepted the extra passenger. Boris seemed to truly enjoy his new status as a rider. He snuggled contentedly in my lap and tried several times to stretch his head up to lick my face. I shoved him lightheartedly back down.

When we got back to the farm and I set him down on the ground he immediately resumed his favorite sport of darting back and forth around Aron's legs. But this time Aron didn't bother to get upset about it. He just stood there and looked at Boris, until Boris got tired of his game and decided to go home. I looked after him, wondering if Anna was going to be afraid of him. Most likely she would, I thought dismally. Anna would probably be scared of everything, from horses to mosquitoes, and ruin my entire summer vacation. Then I remembered Rachel, and my mood lightened again. She and I were going to have some fun rides this summer, regardless of what Anna did or didn't do.

Chapter 2

The next morning I got up early and ran out to the stable, but Rachel had beaten me to it. She was already busy feeding the horses outside in the pasture. Rachel had arrived kind of late the night before, so I hadn't been able to talk to her much yet.

"Hi," I said. "You're quite an early riser, aren't you? Or maybe you stayed up all night?" Rachel smiled her bright smile, while she lifted a fork load of hay in to Pinczow. The beautiful red three-year-old stallion started wolfing down the food greedily. He was equally energetic and temperamental in everything he did. Breaking him in might prove to be more exciting than we would like, I thought to myself. The thing about not sleeping is an old joke between Rachel and me. When we'd visited each other before, we'd often planned to stay up and watch movies and talk about horses and stuff all night. But by the end of the first movie we always fell asleep.

"Oh, no, I fell asleep practically before I got to bed," she assured me, but I thought she looked a little pale and tired. That may be understandable, if it was true that she was sad and lovesick over some boy, I thought. Or could it be the strange phone call last night that had bothered her? The phone had rung just as we were going to bed. Rachel had answered it because she was closest to the phone, and said, "Hello! Johnson residence." Then she had listened for a moment and said, "What do you mean by that?" before she hung up suddenly.

"Who was it?" asked my dad.

"No idea," said Rachel. "Some idiot who doesn't have anything better to do than make crank calls."

"What did he say?" Mom asked curiously.

"Oh, just some nonsense," said Rachel. She seemed kind of tense and serious, I thought.

"He said something like "Nobody does wrong against me unpunished." I had been close enough to Rachel to hear what had been said at the other end. "I think it was a man, even though he spoke in a high-pitched voice."

"It must be some poor, disturbed person," said my mom. "One of those who just calls people randomly to upset them. Nothing to worry about."

Right afterwards we all went to bed, and nobody said anything more about the call. But I'm sure my mom was right, I thought. It had to be some stupid crank call. There was no reason to think the call had anything to do with Rachel. Her being a little quiet and strange afterwards was probably just a coincidence. She was probably tired from the drive. That must also be why she seemed a little tense.

I shook off the unpleasant thoughts and went into Aron's stall. He was waiting impatiently for his breakfast. Did I dare ask Rachel about it? I pondered this while trying to push Aron's muzzle away, as he was eagerly sniffing my hands to see if I had a treat hidden for him. No, I'd better wait until she started talking about it herself.

"Hey, cut that out," I said with a laugh, as Aron tried to bite my hand. "I'll give you food, but you cannot have my fingers for an appetizer, you greedy monster."

Aron looked a little offended, but forgot it quickly when a large armful of sweet-smelling hay landed in front of him. I stood by and watched him while he chowed down on it eagerly. He was so beautiful. I was happy it wasn't I who had to be away from my horse for a whole month. I turned to Rachel.

"What exactly happened to Nùpur?" I asked curiously. "My mom said he was injured, but she didn't know how it happened."

"What happened is almost too stupid to be true," said Rachel as she shook her head. "I was just going to back him out of the horse trailer, and then there was a hole in the ground right next to the loading ramp. If I had only seen it in time! But I didn't. Nùpur stepped right into the hole, and that was that. We were just lucky the injury wasn't more serious than it was. The next time I back him out of a trailer I'll inspect the ground with a magnifying glass first, that's for sure."

I started imagining Rachel crawling around on all fours with a huge magnifying glass in front of her eye, which was such a comical image that I had to giggle, even though I thought it was very sad what had happened to Núpur.

"What are you laughing at?" Rachel wanted to know.

I opened my mouth to tell her when my dad came in. He looked anything but full of laughter.

"I just talked to Cooper on the phone," he said gravely. "There was a fire at their place last night. And everything indicates that someone started it intentionally."

Chapter 3

When Rachel and I went for a horseback ride later on, I was filled with a feeling of doom. The Coopers had a ranch not very far from us. The fire had started in a tool shed adjacent to the animal barn. There were cows in the barn, as well as two riding ponies that belonged to the Coopers' 10-year-old twin daughters.

Luckily the fire had been discovered in time. A taxi driver, who had been on his way home, had seen the flames and called both Mr. Cooper and the emergency number. The fire had come very close to spreading into the animal barn, but everything ended well. Even though the animals had panicked, none of them had been injured. Fortunately they were more frightened than hurt.

Evidently Rachel had been thinking the same as I, because suddenly she said, "It's scary to think how pure coincidence can often determine life or death. If that taxi driver hadn't been driving by right then, fourteen dairy cows and two ponies might very well be dead.

"Yeah, it's pretty scary," I agreed. "But the scariest thing is that someone deliberately set fire to that tool shed. Who on earth would do such a thing? I can't understand it."

"It couldn't have been meant as an ordinary prank," said Rachel as she stroked Baggi, the horse my dad had chosen for her to ride. Baggi is a Shagya Arabian and very good-natured, even though he can be quite a handful sometimes. "Nobody could be so stupid that they didn't understand the danger of igniting a shed that's next to an animal barn," she continued. "I think whoever did it must have actually intended to hurt Mr. Cooper."

We discussed this from horseback, while scanning the pastures. But we didn't come to any conclusions. The thought of somebody deliberately doing such an evil act was incomprehensible to both of us.

After a while, Rachel said, "No, let's talk about more pleasant things." She pointed toward the pasture. "The foals are so adorable! I don't know of any other creatures who have such long legs, and look as sweet and clumsy as Arabian foals. Small foals have this innocent expression on their faces, so unsuspecting and trusting.

I nodded in agreement. "They are the most adorable creatures in the world," I said, and got an irritable snort from Aron as a reply. I started stroking his neck quickly. "After you, of course," I said soothingly. "Nobody is more adorable than you, Aron. You should know that."

But Aron had lost interest. The green grass in front of him was far more interesting than compliments from me. He snatched greedily at some savory straws and gobbled them up.

Baggi followed his example. Rachel patted him. "It sure is different riding Baggi, compared to Nùpur," she said. "Nùpur isn't as tall, of course, but he has a little rounder form, while Baggi seems much taller, and much narrower. But I'm sure I'll get used to him over time."

"Sure you will," I said. "And if not, there are plenty of other horses to choose from, both among our own Arabians and the ones that are spending the summer in our pastures. The owners are only too happy to have them be ridden now and then, so just let us know if you'd like to switch to a different one. Right now we're renting out pasture for Shetland ponies, cold blooded horses and Welsh ponies. I pointed. "You can see one of the Shetland ponies and her foal right over there."

Rachel smiled. "They are so cute," she said. "But I don't think I want to switch horses. I'm sure Baggi and I will get along just fine," she said. "I just have to get used to sitting so high up. It's been a long time since I've ridden anything other than an Icelandic horse, so this feels almost a little scary."

"Well, I'm sure you can share your fears with Anna when she comes," I joked. "Last time she was here, she wasn't only scared of big horses, but every pony, dog and guinea pig she came near."

18

Rachel laughed. "She wasn't actually scared of guinea pigs, was she?" she said as she made Baggi walk and we continued riding.

"I'd bet on it," I said gloomily. "We just didn't come across any. If we had, I'm sure she would have been scared of it, too."

"She may not be such a wimp anymore," said Rachel optimistically. "And if she is, the two of us could always try to break her of it. Toughen her up a bit, if you know what I mean."

"That's actually a good idea," I said, nodding. "But do you think we'd be able to?"

"Oh, I wouldn't find it too impossible," said Rachel. "The fact that the overprotective Aunt Joanne isn't around may just do half the job. Who knows?"

"What do you mean? Overprotective Aunt Joanne?" I glanced over at Rachel.

Rachel nodded. "Haven't you noticed? Last time she visited us – this was before Aunt Joanne got sick – she didn't do anything but warn, warn, warn. 'Put on a sweater, or you might get pneumonia. Don't go near the water – what if you fall in and drown? Don't you dare climb that tree! You could fall down and get seriously injured.' There was no end to her warnings!"

"You know, you're right!" I said, astonished. "That's how she kept on last time she was here, too. I guess I just haven't thought about it before. No wonder Anna is so scared of everything!"

"Well, let's work really hard at de-scaring her," said Rachel with determination. "But let's talk about something more interesting, like racing, for example. Last one to the edge of the woods is a rotten egg!"

I didn't need to be asked twice, and neither did Aron. Racing is his favorite thing to do, and he hates to lose. But when we got to the edge of the woods, he was a couple of horse lengths behind Baggi. I just laughed and thought it was fun anyway.

Just as I was about to turn Aron around to ride across the meadow, I noticed someone walking in the woods. It was kind of dark under the trees, so it was hard to tell if it was a man or a woman, but I was pretty sure it was a man. When the person saw us, he

19

stopped abruptly and stood completely still. His strange behavior made me curious. In a low voice I made Rachel aware of the person in between the trees. She threw a quick glance in the direction I had indicated, and then said, "I don't like this. Let's get away from here."

I was surprised by her reaction, but obeyed and turned Aron around. Then we trotted vigorously back home.

I tried to ask Rachel why she had reacted so strongly to the person in the woods, but she gave only a short answer, that she didn't like people who sneaked around and watched others.

Afterwards she seemed quiet and reserved, giving only one-word responses when I talked to her. I could see that the person in the woods had scared her, but didn't know why, and I didn't want to ask her, not yet anyway.

Her mood rubbed off on me, and I caught myself looking around for strangers and sneaking figures behind every bush. I told myself this was idiotic, but I couldn't get rid of the feeling that something was wrong. I had no idea what it was. It was just a feeling I had, and I suspected that Rachel felt the same thing. She turned frequently to throw searching glances behind us, as if she expected to be followed.

Chapter 4

Anna had not changed. She was of course taller and looked more grown up than before. After all, it had been two years since I saw her. But the anxious look and her whiny voice were still the same. Well, maybe not quite the same, but bad enough to make me feel irritated by the way she looked around in all directions of the farmyard with a frightened look. It was like she expected to be attacked by some monster at any moment.

She backed up slightly toward the front door of the house when Dad came walking toward us with Pinczow on a tether. And she could not hide her relief when Dad just cheerfully shouted, " Hi and welcome!" as he continued walking toward the stable with the horse. Before he got there Boris showed up, delightedly in the mood for another bout with one of those four-legged giants that were so amusing to play with. Barking excitedly, he ran toward Pinczow and started snatching playfully at his legs. But Pinczow was not in the mood to tolerate this irritating, barking, bushy little thing today. He kicked irritatedly at the little pest with his hooves. Fortunately he didn't hit Boris with full force, but one of the hooves grazed him enough to make the poor dog squeal in pain and run away with his tail between his legs. When he came scampering over to us for comfort and support, it was Anna's turn to squeal.

"Help, it's getting me!" she screamed and ran toward the front door as fast as her legs could carry her.

Mom quickly scooped Boris up, as he trembled and whimpered and wagged his tail all at once. Rachel and I helped hold him, as my mom ran her hands all across his body to examine him.

Finally she straightened up and said with relief, "No harm done. He just got a sock and a shock, so to speak."

21

"Maybe this will teach him a lesson," commented Rachel, who now seemed like her old, lively self again. "He might stay away from the horses after this."

"I doubt it," said Mom laughingly. "This isn't the first time this has happened, and it never scared him off for more than one or two days at the most. After a while he just can't stand it any longer, and starts playing around with them again."

After plenty of petting and cuddling and comforting, Boris went on home, wagging his tail contentedly. It didn't look like his violent clash with Pinczow had hurt him noticeably, so I was pretty sure Mom would be right about it not taking long before he resumed his dangerous game.

Dutifully Rachel and I went inside to talk to Anna. All my worst suspicions had been confirmed, it seemed. Anna was every bit the scaredy cat she had been last time she was here. What would the rest of this summer vacation be like, I wondered while I stepped into the hall and closed the door behind me.

Chapter 5

"How cute they are!" said Anna reverently, while she watched the foals at a safe distance as they jumped around in a lively and disorganized game.

Anna had, surprisingly, let us talk her into walking down to the pasture with us after dinner, to look at the foals. During the meal, we talked about the fire again. The police had confirmed that the fire had in fact been set intentionally. Anna was as shocked as we were when she learned how narrowly they had escaped a real catastrophy.

"The foals are incredibly tame and trusting," said Rachel with a smile to Anna. "Would you like to pet one of them?"

Anna nodded hesitantly, and I called Niobe, Grenada's foal, over to us. Niobe approached us with curiosity, tottering on her long, slim legs. I stroked her calmingly over her soft foal coat and coaxed her over toward Rachel and Anna. Anna threw suspicious glances over toward Grenada, who was grazing peacefully and didn't seem to worry about us at all. Anna stroked her hand carefully along Niobe's back. Niobe turned her head and looked at Anna with her dark, innocent eyes. Very cautiously Anna stroked the filly foal's forehead and muzzle. Niobe neighed happily and stuck her muzzle into her hand. Anna jerked slightly, but even she realized that Niobe in no way could be considered dangerous, and soon she was completely absorbed by this sweet little heartbreaker. Niobe thoroughly enjoyed being scratched and patted. Rachel and I were so preoccupied by the interaction between Anna and the foal that we didn't notice Grenada, who had started worrying about her offspring. We didn't see her coming until she stuck her head down in between us to sniff her foal and check that everything was in order.

When Anna discovered the big horse head right in front of her, she screamed so loudly that I'm sure they could hear it miles away. I don't know who got the biggest shock, Rachel and I, or Grenada and Niobe, but we all jumped at the sound of the unexpected scream.

"It's going to bite me! Get it away!" wailed Anna and scrambled to her feet in a hurry.

Poor little Niobe was scared out of her mind by this strange, howling creature. She backed away, turned abruptly, stumbled over her own legs and fell in the grass. There she stayed, looking astonished at Anna's fleeing figure.

I didn't know whether to laugh or be angry. Anna had behaved completely idiotically, I thought. At the same time the sight of Niobe struggling to get her long, thin legs under control again was so comical that it wasn't possible to stay serious. I walked over to her, stroked her head, and helped her up. A moment later she ran off, jumping happily, and had apparently forgotten all about the scare she just had. Grenada followed her little foal at a calmer pace.

I turned toward Rachel, who was still sitting in the grass. She laughed so hard she was crying. "Did you see Anna's face?" she said when she was finally able to speak. She wiped away a tear and continued: "I know it's not very nice of me to laugh at her. That poor thing, how scared she was! But that scream, and the speed with which she scrambled to her feet, that's just one of the funniest things I've seen in a long time."

"But someone could have gotten hurt, the way she acted, scaring the horses half to death!" I said, feeling my anger returning. "How could that have been something to get so hysterical about? I mean, she wasn't attacked by Grenada or anything! I swear, Anna is completely hopeless!"

Rachel shook her head. "I don't believe she is hopeless," she said. "But evidently she has a fear of large animals."

"You don't say!" I uttered sarcastically. "I hadn't noticed. Just imagine what a great summer vacation we'll have if that stupid girl is going to scream every time she sees a horse. There are horses all over this place, in case you hadn't noticed. So what are we

24

going to do? Let her sit inside all day, or pull a paper bag over her head? That way she won't see these scary monsters!"

"I vote for the paper bag," laughed Rachel. "But let's be serious," she said, "I think we should try to help Anna get over this fear. It couldn't possibly be much fun to live this way."

"I just cannot understand how it's possible to be scared of something as beautiful as a horse!" I exclaimed.

"Well, to Anna they are evidently more scary than beautiful," Rachel said. "About as scary as snakes are to you."

I shuddered. Snakes are the most disgusting creatures I know of. "But certainly you can't compare the two," I objected. "Horses are pretty. Snakes are frightening and horrible!"

"Well, my pen pal in England sure doesn't think so," said Rachel. "Her name is Debbie, and her brother has two large boas for pets. At first she refused to be in the same room as the snakes, but now they're the coolest things in the world, according to her."

I shuddered again. Of course I knew that some people have spiders, snakes and even small crocodiles for pets, but personally I didn't understand how they could think of these creatures as cute.

"Imagine that you were going to stay at my place for a month," said Rachel, "and that I had a house full of big snakes that I expected you to pet and get excited about."

"Are you saying that the horses are just as scary and frightening to Anna as the snakes would have been to me?" I said slowly, trying to let this new way of looking at the problem sink in.

Rachel nodded. "We will simply have to get her used to the horses in small doses, step by step, muzzle by muzzle," she said. "Remember that Anna is not behaving this way in order to be mean or difficult. She simply cannot control her fear."

"Alright," I said, "I will try to be more patient with her. Maybe we can talk her into coming with us to the stable? In there the horses are locked up in their stalls and can't run after her, or whatever she imagines that they'll do."

"Good idea," said Rachel. "But I think we'd better wait until tomorrow before we suggest it. I bet Anna has had enough excitement for one day."

Chapter 6

"There's been another fire in the neighborhood!"

"Hmmm? What? Who?" I sat up in bed, still feeling dizzy and drowsy. I had been dreaming about fleeing horses and mysterious phone calls, and for a moment I didn't know if the voice was real or part of my dream. But then I woke up. Mom stood in the doorway, and this was no dream.

"Another fire? Where?"

"At the Thompson ranch. Their barn burned to the ground last night, and it was arson again!"

I felt a chill go through me. I knew that the Thompsons had both sheep and horses. The sheep were in the summer pasture right now, of course, but the horses, what had happened to them? I didn't know if I dared ask, but my mom knew what I was thinking and quickly reassured me that the horses had been outside in the pastures too, so the barn had been empty.

All kinds of thoughts were buzzing through my head while I dressed as fast as I could. Who could this person be, who was sneaking around and setting fire to other people's property in the middle of the night? What could the motive be, and where would he strike the next time? If there was a mentally sick pyromaniac in town, anyone could be his next victim. Just the thought of it made me sick with fear. What if he came here? What if he set fire to our stable?

I looked from Rachel to Anna. We had talked about nothing but the fire since we came out to the stable after breakfast, and I'm sure it was the tenth time I was expressing my worst fear.

Rachel twisted her face into something that was probably supposed to be a reassuring smile, but it was merely a grimace. I looked at her searchingly. She seemed tired and out of sorts. The night before there had been another anonymous phone call. Rachel, who happened to be walking by the phone when it rang, had answered it, listened for a moment and then slammed the receiver back on the hook. When I asked who it was, she had just said it was someone calling the wrong number. Then she had said goodnight and gone straight to bed.

I didn't believe for a second that it was a wrong number. Rachel's behavior told me otherwise. What exactly was going on? Did the same person who had called before called again? Did Rachel know who was calling? I thought about the incident in the woods, where Rachel had acted kind of strange, as if she was scared. What was bothering her? Or rather, who was bothering her?

I decided to have a talk with her and try to find out as soon as possible, because what if...

Anna's voice interrupted my thoughts. "Do you think we should keep watch around the stable tonight?" she asked. "I mean, if there's a crazy pyromaniac on the loose, you never know when he will strike again, or where."

Anna looked at me expectantly, then threw a quick, anxious glance over her shoulder at the sound of one of the horses who was neighing inside his stall. I concentrated on suppressing the irritation I felt. Think about snakes, I said to myself. Remember that to Anna, that horse is a snake! It actually helped, because when I focused my thoughts on my own big fear, it was easier to understand Anna's.

Rachel and I had used every ounce of persuasive skills that we possessed in order to talk Anna into coming to the stable with us at all. At last she had reluctantly given in, and it had actually gone pretty well so far. At least she hadn't fled in panic yet, which is something, I thought to myself.

"I definitely agree we need some kind of watch by the stable," said Rachel, and I nodded too. "But right now we'd better get started feeding and cleaning stalls around here, before the horses start neighing their little hearts out from plain impatience," she went on, pointing at the closest stalls where restless muzzles were being pressed against the bars and big, brown horse eyes looked at us with anticipation.

I was glad to see Rachel's smile was more natural and relaxed now. Soon we were hard at work. Anna had volunteered to be the wheelbarrow driver. That way she didn't have to be in close contact with the horses. Rachel and I loaded the wheelbarrow with used bedding, and she wheeled load after load out to the waste pile. When we were done, I managed to convince her to come over to Quatana, the calmest and most mild-mannered horse on the whole farm. Anna stood there and watched Quatana for quite a while, with a skeptical expression on her face. Quatana glanced over at us a few times from inside her stall, but concentrated mostly on the thing that all horses are most fond of, which is eating.

When Quatana lifted her head and pressed her muzzle against the bars of the door, Anna jumped back a little, but she didn't run away.

"See the kind look in those eyes," I said quietly, and pointed at Quatana. "There isn't a trace of evil in that horse."

"But she's so big," whispered Anna.

"Big and friendly," I said. "She wouldn't hurt you for the world. And she loves to be patted and cuddled with. Would you like to scratch her forehead?"

"But what if she bites me?"

"Quatana doesn't bite," I said confidently. "You can be quite sure of that. Some of the stallions might bite sometimes, but never Quatana."

I carefully took Anna's hand and lifted it toward Quatana's head. I was prepared for her to jerk her arm back, but ever so carefully she stretched her arm in between the bars and scratched the top of Quatana's forehead, as far from the muzzle as she could get. Quatana flapped her ears and looked like she enjoyed it. Anna scratched her a little more, then withdrew her arm and smiled.

"Well done!" said Rachel's voice from behind us. "You are brave, Anna!"

Anna looked at her, surprised. "I am not brave," she said. "I'm

28

such a sissy, I'm ashamed of myself. Don't you think I know? After I ran away from the pasture yesterday, I could have died of shame because I'd behaved so idiotically. I really appreciated it when neither of you mentioned a word about it after you got home."

"Of course you're brave," said Rachel. "You just did something you're scared to do, and that takes courage. Taking the elevator to the top of the Eiffel Tower is nothing to a person who isn't scared of heights, but if you do have a fear of heights, it takes courage to overcome your fears and do that."

Anna looked happy, and I was thinking to myself that Rachel was right. It's no big deal to do something you're not scared of at all. Anna had taken a small step today toward overcoming her fears. Maybe we could even get her up on a horse before summer break was over? That would be fun.

"Would you join me for a ride?" I asked Rachel a little later. "You and I can ride the horses, and Anna could ride my bike. That is, if you want to, I added, turning to Anna."

"Sorry, I promised your mom to help her exercise some horses," said Rachel. "This is a paid summer job, you know!"

"You poor thing!" I said teasingly. "Having to slave away in the stable."

Rachel laughed and threw a sponge at me. "Maybe I can come along for a ride later," she said. "But you and Anna can still go, can't you?"

I looked over at Anna. She nodded slowly. "I could go," she said, "if you'll chose a route where I can ride the bike, that is. I don't think I'm quite ready to ride a horse yet!"

We all laughed. "I'll be happy to give you some riding lessons," said Rachel. "Just let me know when you feel ready to try."

"We'll see," said Anna evasively and squirmed. "I'll have to get used to being around the horses first."

"Well, then a bike ride with Eva and Aron should be a nice start," stated Rachel. "You get to be near a horse, but still keep your distance."

"Ah, this is the good life!" I said happily a little later, as Anna and I turned onto a nice, flat forest trail that was suitable for both horseback riding and biking.

"Phew! Speak for yourself," sighed Anna. "If there's one more uphill, I'm going to die from heat exhaustion, just so you know!"

I turned around and looked at her. Her face was deep red from exertion. "See how much smarter it is to ride a horse," I said, grinning. "You just let the horse know where you want to go, and he'll do the hard part. No need to tread pedals to get up a hill. But you can relax, from here on it's flat. You can just cancel that heat stroke."

Anna took a breath of relief. She was biking right next to Aron and me now. At first she had stayed a good distance behind us, but she had gradually come closer, seemingly without even noticing. It seemed that she was already in the process of getting over her worst fear of horses. I hoped so.

"Look, there's a hunter walking in there!" said Anna suddenly.

I turned my head to look in the direction she was pointing. At first I didn't see anything other than trees and bushes, but then I discovered a man wearing a camouflage outfit. He was carrying something – was it a gun? I strained my eyes to see better. No, it wasn't a gun...it was binoculars. Just then the man saw us. He immediately turned his back and set off into the woods as quick as a cricket.

Anna and I looked at each other. What a strange way to behave! It was almost as if he had something to hide.

"I thought for a moment that he meant to shoot us," laughed Anna nervously. "Some imagination I have! Maybe I read too many mystery books."

"Well, I kind of jumped too," I said. "Until I saw he was carrying binoculars, and not a gun."

"Do you think he might have been one of those bird watchers?" wondered Anna. "They often sit around motionless for hours in order to get a glimpse of a rare hawk or something."

"I guess it's possible, but I don't see why he would run off like that just because we showed up. Why would he do that, if he didn't have something to hide?"

Suddenly I remembered the mysterious figure who'd been standing amongst the trees and watching Rachel and me the day before. Could it be the same person? If so, what was he up to? Why sneak around in the woods with binoculars? A thought came to me. What if...

"What if it's the fire starter, lurking about looking for another place to set on fire?" I said, frightened by the thought.

Anna thought for a while. "Are there any houses or ranches in those woods?" she wanted to know.

I shook my head. "But it is a pretty smart place to move around if you don't want to be seen by anyone. Regardless of where you come out from the woods, you'll have a view of somebody's house or ranch."

I decided to tell Mom and Dad about this when we got home. The man was probably there on a completely innocent errand, but still, his behavior was so suspicious that I just couldn't leave it at that.

Chapter 7

On the way home, I gave Anna a headstart on her bike before I set off in pursuit of her on Aron. He really enjoyed galloping, so we caught up with Anna pretty quickly and slowed down again. Anna smiled and gave Aron a quick pat on the flank, but withdrew her hand again just as fast.

Rachel met us in the farmyard when we got back. She was smiling and looking cheerful, but her good mood vanished instantly when we told her what we had seen in the woods.

She wanted to know if we'd seen the man's face, and if we could tell about how old he was. I thought her questions were a little strange, but neither Anna nor I had seen the man's face, so we had no idea how old he could be.

Rachel mumbled something that I didn't understand and went inside the house. I stared after her with my mouth open. What on earth was going on with her? Did she have some idea who the man was and what he was doing in the woods? If so, why wouldn't she tell us?

Dad thought we had probably just seen an innocent hiker, but he still wanted to keep watch by the stable that night. "After all, there have been two cases of arson in the neighborhood the last couple of days," he said, "so I don't see any reason to take chances."

Later in the afternoon, when Rachel and I were going for a ride, I tried to question her. Anna had stayed home to watch some TV show she liked, and I thought I'd take advantage of the opportunity while I had Rachel to myself.

I wasn't sure how to approach the issue about the mysterious man. But Rachel gave me a perfect excuse. When I suggested that we ride in the woods, she blankly refused.

"Why not?" I asked her. "What are you afraid of? Is it that man we saw? Do you know him? Is he the one who's been calling two nights in a row? What does he want? Is he dangerous? Do you think he might be the arsonist?"

Rachel refused to answer my questions. "I don't know," she said reluctantly. "I... I... need time to think. The whole thing is just too crazy."

That was all she would say. We kept silent for the rest of the ride. Rachel seemed distant and preoccupied, so I left her alone, even though I was dying for answers.

Instead I tried to concentrate on Aron and the ride. Aron was spunky and happy, and seemed to think it was great to do two rides in the same day. But for the first time I wasn't able to enjoy a ride on my favorite horse. Too many unpleasant thoughts were crossing my mind: thoughts about mysterious people, threatening phone calls and scary fires.

On the way home we rode past the Hansen house. It looked so sad and abandoned, without roof pans, just waiting to be torn down. There was still glass in the windows, and for a moment I thought I saw someone moving behind one of them, but it must have been just a reflection that played a trick on my eyes.

That night I had one of the worst nightmares I have ever had. I dreamed that I was keeping watch in the stable, which was not in our barn. It was an elegant, long, white wooden building. While I was inside the stable, a horrible, six-and-a-half-foot tall man in a camouflage suit showed up. He used his binoculars to nail the door shut, locking me in.

My mom and dad sat outside the stable, having coffee and chatting. I screamed and hollered for help, but they didn't hear me. They just sat there discussing how many roof pans should be on the Hansen house, and how good it would be when the police had arrested the arsonist. "Just think of all the smoke that's emitted by such fires," I heard Mom say. "It can't possibly be safe for the environment. It was smart of Hansen to move somewhere else. They really ought to have a law against fires!"

"Help! Help!" I yelled, as the man in the camouflage suit poured gasoline from a huge jug all around the stable. But nobody heard me, and suddenly Mom and Dad were gone. The farmyard was totally deserted and flames started creeping up the walls. The horses panicked, and so did I. I tried to open the windows, but every time I touched a window latch, the window disappeared and instead there was just a hard, unbreakable concrete wall. Then, as if by magic, the roof was lifted off the stable. It doesn't help, I thought frantically. The horses can't climb all the way up there. But they didn't need to. Suddenly, large wings unfolded on their backs, and they flew up, out of the stable and into the night. I stood there, left all alone, calling out for Aron to come back for me and save me, but he didn't hear. He was just flying elegantly away with powerful strokes of his wings. When I turned again, the figure in the camouflage suit was standing right in front of me, and a deep voice said: "Nobody does wrong against me unpunished!"

He reached his hands out for me threateningly. Terror-stricken, I pulled back, fell off a cliff, and in the next instant, I woke up lying on the floor in my room. I had fallen out of my bed. I scrambled to my feet and squinted at the clock. It was 5:30. I might as well get dressed and go to the stable. I definitely didn't want to go back to sleep for fear that the nightmare would come back.

When I went into the kitchen, I found Dad sitting there eating breakfast. He looked tired, and was planning to sleep a few hours after he'd eaten. I half expected him to tell me that the arsonist had tried at our stable, but everything had been quiet, Dad said.

Rachel padded into the room, yawning really wide. She looked as if she was only half awake.

"Hi there," said Dad, as he smiled at her. "You look more tired than I do, sweetheart! Haven't you slept at all?"

"Yes, I have, just not long enough," said Rachel as she shivered. "But I'll wake up gradually."

34

"Well, you could go outside and get the paper if you want," suggested Dad. "The fresh air might wake you up."

"I'll do that," smiled Rachel and disappeared out the door. A little while later we heard her come back, but she didn't return to the kitchen. She went past the kitchen door and upstairs instead. It was quite a while before she showed up with the paper, and then she looked even more tired and drawn.

Dad looked at her searchingly, and was about to say something, but Rachel spoke first.

"Do we have anything special on the schedule for today?" she asked quickly. "For the horses, I mean."

"Mainly the usual," said Dad. "But I was thinking of something that might be good for Anna."

Rachel and I looked at him curiously.

"We could put her in charge of one of the foals. She could take care of it, get it used to being led on a tether, get it used to a bridle, lift its legs and check them, and all the usual stuff. Do you think she would like that?"

"Yes, I'm sure she would," I said. "She really liked Niobe, so maybe she could take care of her? I think she'll do fine, because she's not quite as scared anymore."

Anna got all excited about Dad's offer. The only thing that made her a little skeptical was what she would do if Grenada came too close. But Dad didn't think that should be a problem. If Anna thought things got a little scary, she could just quietly and slowly leave the pasture. Before taking his much desired nap, Dad walked Anna down to the pasture and showed her what to do.

Rachel and I went to the stable and started the morning chores. Mom stuck her head inside the door and said hello.

It made me start, because for an instant I thought she had come to tell us about some new fire in the neighborhood. But she just wanted to know if we could manage the stable work by ourselves, as she wanted to go to the office and get some accounting work out of the way. We just waved her off.

Rachel wasn't very talkative that morning, but I decided to ig-

35

nore it, and chatted away about horses and horse care and how nice it was that all our newborn foals seemed to be healthy and strong this year. Rachel loosened up gradually, and we kept to safe topics the whole time we worked.

After we were done in the stable, we agreed to take Aron and Baggi outside to groom them, and then take a little ride. While we were doing this, Anna returned from the pasture and told us excitedly how fantastic Niobe had been. She had obviously fallen head over heels in love with the foal. I smiled happily and was just about to say something encouraging to Anna when Boris showed up. He had stayed away since his clash with Pinczow, but now he was evidently ready to play again.

He ran excitedly across the farmyard and straight for Anna. Actually it was Aron and Baggi he was aiming for, but Anna thought he was going to attack her. In shock, she took a few steps backward.

"Watch out for the grooming box!" I screamed, but it was too late.

Anna stepped right into the grooming box, lost her balance and fell backward, right under Aron's belly!

I held my breath. Surely this was going to end in disaster, I thought. Aron had not moved an inch yet, but if Anna panicked and started wailing and screaming, or if Boris started snapping at Aron's legs... I didn't dare finish the thought.

Rachel made a desperate attempt to stop Boris, but he slipped elegantly out of her reach and threw himself delightedly at the horses. With piercing barks he flew into Aron's forelegs. He didn't bite, just pretended, but at any moment I expected Aron to start stomping his forelegs or throwing kicks at the irritating, noisy troublemaker. To my surprise, Aron did neither. He looked down at Anna who was lying underneath his belly, and it looked like he understood that he had to be careful right now.

Anna didn't move either. At first I thought she had hurt herself, but then I decided she must be paralyzed with fear.

The whole thing lasted only a few seconds, but it seemed like an eternity. Rachel succeeded in grabbing Boris. She lifted him up, holding him in a firm grip, even though he wriggled like crazy to get free.

I bent down and pulled Anna to her feet. I could feel her whole body trembling. Oh darn, everything is ruined, I thought. Thanks to Boris, Anna will be more frightened than ever. She probably wouldn't go near a horse ever again. I could tell by Rachel's face that she was thinking the same thing. But then Anna took us both by complete surprise. She walked right over to Aron and stroked his neck.

"Did you see how fantastic he was?" she said to Rachel and me, and we nodded, perplexed, unsure what she meant.

"That stupid dog was running around trying to bite him, and even though I'm sure he wanted to trample Boris, he stood quite still, just to protect me. I would never have thought a horse could be that intelligent, and kind!"

Rachel and I looked unbelievingly at each other. This was far from the reaction we had been expecting. Instead of increasing Anna's fear, it seemed as though the startling event had removed it! How strange! It seemed like she suddenly understood that the horse is a friendly animal and not a life-threatening creature waiting for an opportunity to attack her. Now she was standing by Aron and scratching his forehead as if it was the most natural thing for her to do.

She wasn't quite as confident an hour later, however, while sitting on the back of a horse for the first time. We had decided to strike while the iron was hot, and her fears cold. But Anna was sitting on top of the kind and peaceful Quatana, stiff as a stick and holding on to the horse's mane with a grip so tight her knuckles were white. Rachel and I stood on either side of her to help and give support.

"You're doing just fine!" said Rachel. "Try to relax a little. Quatana won't do anything unexpected. I promise you!"

"I'm try... trying," said Anna, her teeth clattering from sheer fright.

I felt sorry for her. We just stood there for a while, saying encouraging things to her before we started leading Quatana gently and slowly around in a walk. Quatana was so calm and walked at such a leisurely pace, that after only one round Anna had loosened her grip on the mane a little. After a few more rounds, Rachel coaxed her to take the reins.

"But what if I fall down?" said Anna, frightened.

"I will walk right next to you and catch you if you do," I said quickly. "And even if you did fall out of the saddle, the riding ground is so soft that you wouldn't get hurt. All the riders fall off the horse now and then. It's part of riding, kind of."

At the end of the improvised riding lesson, Anna sat quite nicely in the saddle, and she definitely didn't look as scared anymore. Rachel and I praised her a lot, and she had to admit that it hadn't really been so bad, sitting on a horse.

"Just wait until you've had a few more riding lessons," said Rachel, "then you'll just love it."

"I'll ask my mom to teach you," I said enthusiastically. "She's a wonderful riding instructor. And Rachel and I will help you as much as we can. I promise you that by the end of this vacation you'll be going on horseback rides with us!"

Chapter 8

Mom felt it was a good idea to give Anna her first riding lesson that same afternoon. While she and Anna worked together, I helped Rachel lead Assisam, one of our yearlings. Assisam is a really boisterous little rascal who had no intention of walking nicely next to Rachel on a tether. No matter how much Rachel coaxed and demonstrated, he flatly refused to walk nicely. It was a lot more fun to bolt forward, throw himself to the side or run over toward me to check if I had treats in my pockets. In the end Rachel was sweaty and exhausted, while I laughed so hard I had to hold my belly.

"Here, you do it, if you think you're such an expert," said Rachel, holding the rope challengingly over toward me.

"No thank you," I said between gasps. "It's a lot more fun to watch. This is almost better than the circus!"

Rachel stuck her tongue out at me, but she laughed along. Finally she actually did get Assisam to do a short distance of something that with a good stretch of the imagination could be called a nice walk. Assisam received tons of praise and pats, and was released into the pasture. He ran off with his tail up, looking quite proud of himself.

"It's always a good idea to stop when things are going reasonably well," said Rachel with a grin. I nodded in agreement and asked if she wanted to go for a ride in the nice weather. But Rachel had more work to do, so she suggested that Anna and I go without her.

"But do you think Anna can ride like that already?" I asked stupidly.

"No, no," laughed Rachel, "I was thinking she could ride the bike again, like yesterday."

"No, thanks anyway," said Anna when I asked her a little later. She patted her behind. "I've discovered some new muscles here," she said with a grimace. "And they all hurt. Not for the life of me would I sit on a bike seat right now."

I laughed, but felt a little disappointed. It would have been fun with some company on my ride. Mom was coming out of the stable and had heard what Anna said.

"I have an idea," she said. "If you and Anna will help me in the kitchen for half an hour, then I'll take over Rachel's job afterward, and the two of you can go for a real ride. Rachel is supposed to have a little fun while she's here too, you know, not just work."

"Mom, you're an angel!" I said, hugging her. "I'll even volunteer to peel the potatoes!"

Then I suddenly thought of Anna. "What are you going to do while we're gone?" I asked. "Won't it be boring for you if Rachel and I go for a ride?"

Anna shook her head. "Not at all," she said. "I can help your mom in the stable, or I might go down to the pasture and play with Niobe for a while. You can relax, there's plenty to do here, just as long as I don't have to sit!" She pointed expressively at her behind, and we all laughed.

Chapter 9

"That poor little house, how deserted and pitiful it looks," uttered Rachel.

We were riding past the Hansen house, which was stripped of all its roof pans. The windows were kind of reflecting the emptiness inside.

"I almost think it looks a little scary," I said with a shiver. "When I see a deserted house like that, I always get the feeling that it's not empty after all, that someone is in there watching me as soon as I turn my back. I'll be glad when the house is gone," I added. "I don't want anything to be left, reminding me of that man who was so horribly cruel to his animals."

Rachel already knew about Randall Hansen, and she agreed with me.

As we continued riding toward the public trail, Rachel turned around in the saddle and looked back at the house again. "Golly," she said, laughing nervously. "I think that vivid imagination of yours is contagious. Just now I got this weird feeling that someone is in there watching us."

I turned and looked at the house, but no matter how much I strained my eyes, I saw only empty glass panes staring blindly and lifelessly back at me. Even so I felt a shiver down my spine. To counteract the unpleasant feeling, I turned my gaze forward, leaning down and scratching Aron's mane. He snorted loudly and shook his head. I shook my own head at myself as well. There was no end to my ridiculous fantasies. Of course there was nobody in the Hansen house. Who would be? A ghost?

Rachel had been in a good mood the whole time until we approached the woods. She got more and more quiet the closer we got to the trees, and finally she said, "You may call me dumb and hysterical, but I will not go into the woods."

"But why not?" I demanded to know. "Is it because of that guy Anna and I saw? The one we thought might be the arsonist?"

Rachel wouldn't answer at first, but I didn't let her off the hook. This time I wanted to know what was bothering her.

I signaled for Aron to stop, and he immediately started eating the grass. Reluctantly Rachel followed my example. I patted Aron's neck while looking urgingly at Rachel.

"I don't know if your mom told you that it wasn't only because of the summer job that I wanted to come and stay here for a while," she said, hesitating.

I nodded. "She mentioned something about problems with a guy. I thought maybe a boyfriend had broken up with you or something."

"If only it were that simple!" sighed Rachel.

And then I got the whole story. Rachel had been going on a few dates with a guy who was a senior in high school. His name was Roy, and in the beginning Rachel had liked him just fine, but only as a friend. Roy, however, had been extremely intense, said Rachel. After just the first date, he had told her she was the love of his life. Rachel thought this was very embarrassing, since she wasn't in love with him.

She had tried to tell Roy that he was moving too fast, and that they needed to get to know each other first, but he didn't see it that way. He started behaving as though he owned Rachel, and it ended with her telling him they'd better not see each other anymore.

"But he refused to accept that," said Rachel sadly. "He continued to call me and come by my house. He even called my best friend, wanting her to talk me into getting back together with him again. That's when she let it slip that I was planning to go here in order to get away from him. Before I left, he came by my house and told me that I would never get away from him, and that I would be sorry that I had rejected him. And as soon as I got here, the phone calls started. I know it's him calling, even if the voice sounds different."

"You think he's distorting his voice?" I asked. "But then you can't know for sure it's Roy. It could just be a crank caller who picked our number at random. He might even be calling several people, bothering all of them."

Rachel shook her head. "I'm pretty sure it's Roy," she said.

"Okay, let's assume you're right. But even if it's him calling, that doesn't mean he's around here. He could be anywhere."

"It's not just the phone calls," said Rachel quietly. "I was so relieved when he didn't call last night. I thought maybe he'd given up. But this morning I found this on the doormat by the front door. This proves that he's around here somewhere." She pulled out a crimpled, grayish white envelope from her pocket. I noticed the envelope had no stamp, and there was nothing written on it. Inside the envelope was a single white sheet of paper, on which was written in large upper case letters: "You will pay for what you did. Nobody does wrong against me unpunished." The writing was clumsy and uneven. It looked like something a first grader might have done.

"He probably wrote it with his left hand, so that nobody would recognize his handwriting," said Rachel.

"He must be completely insane, if he's following you this way," I said, shocked. "What if he's dangerous? Why didn't you say anything about this earlier?" I stared accusingly at her.

Rachel shrugged her shoulders helplessly. "I didn't know what to do," she said. "It seems completely unreal for Roy to be terrorizing me just because I refused to be his girlfriend. But I can't find any other explanation for what's happening, and that's why I don't want to ride in the woods. What if he suddenly shows up? I'm pretty sure the person you and Anna saw was Roy. I know he has one of those camouflage jackets. And if he has binoculars too, that means he's sneaking around spying on me. It scares me."

"If you're right about your suspicion, it was probably him we saw in the woods the first day you and I were out riding too. You have to tell Mom and Dad. It's not normal for someone to behave this way. You don't know what he might do!"

I looked at her urgently. "Promise me that you'll talk to Mom and Dad about it!"

"I promise," said Rachel. "It was stupid of me to not say anything before, but I was hoping that if I ignored it, he would get tired of it and stop bothering me."

We turned the horses away from the woods and rode home in silence. A myriad of thoughts were swarming in my head. So much had happened in such a short period of time. Was it a mere coincidence that arson and terrorizing phone calls and written threats were happening all at the same time, or was there a connection between them? What if it was Roy who had set the fires in the neighborhood? But why would he do that? Maybe he was simply raving mad and was doing it for fun. The thought made me shudder.

I almost blurted out my suspicions to Rachel, but stopped myself. It sounded too stupid. Even if Rachel was right about Roy following her, it wasn't very likely he had anything to do with the fires. I decided it had to be a coincidence that the two things were happening at the same time.

Chapter 10

The next morning, I got up early. I hadn't thought I would be able to sleep at all last night, as full as my head was with everything that had happened. But I'd slept like a rock, with not even an inkling of a nightmare.

Rachel kept her promise and told my mom and dad about Roy's threats, and about suspecting him of being behind the mysterious phone calls. Mom was quite shocked by the letter Rachel had found. The phone rang while she was still holding it in her hands. The sound made us all jump. My dad answered it and said his name. While he was listening to what was being said at the other end, I noticed that his eyebrows pulled together into an angry wrinkle. Then he said: "If you don't quit this nonsense, I'll contact the poli... Hello? Hello?"

The caller had evidently hung up while my dad talked. Dad told us the caller had said exactly the same as the letter; "You will pay for what you did. Nobody does wrong against me unpunished."

Mom asked him to call the police and tell them about the phone threats, and he did. The police made a note of it, but said there was little they could do for now. If the calls continued, we could possibly get the phone line tapped.

Dad thanked them for their help, though I had no idea why. As far as I could tell, they hadn't helped us in the slightest. Didn't they understand that Rachel might be in danger? Did something terrible have to happen before they took it seriously?

When I got down to the kitchen, Dad was sitting by the table with a cup of coffee and the newspaper. He had kept watch in the stable last night too, without having seen a shadow of anything suspicious.

"Maybe there won't be any more fires," he said optimistically. "I sure hope so. But I intend to keep watch in the stable a few more nights regardless. We can't take any chances. It doesn't sound like the police have any clues for tracking down this madman."

Then the phone rang. "Who on earth could that be this early in the morning?" he wondered as he picked up the phone.

When I heard him exclaim: "I'll be..." I assumed it was another phone threat, but when Dad continued by saying "When did it happen? Did anyone get hurt?" I understood it was something else.

While Dad listened to what the caller was saying, Mom came in, followed by Anna and Rachel. All three looked curiously at Dad, who stood there with a face like a stone, glaring into the air. When he hung up, he said gravely, "One of the stables at the riding school burned down last night. Apparently there's no doubt that it was arson this time too, because they found a gasoline can right by the foundation."

I started feeling sick. What about the horses? What had happened to them?

Before I got the words out, Anna beat me to it. "Were there horses in the stable?" she asked. "What happened to them?"

Dad sat down heavily at the table. "They managed to get them out," he said. "But two of the ponies were hurt in the panic that arose, and had to be taken to the animal hospital. The others apparently got off with minor injuries and will recover. As for the two ponies, they don't know yet."

I felt as if someone had hit me with a sledgehammer in the chest. Two ponies... badly hurt... all because of some crazy person who was going berserk. They might have to be put to sleep... but no, I didn't want to think the worst. The veterinarian would have put them down immediately if there were no hope, wouldn't he?

It was three gloomy girls who were sitting in the pasture a little later, watching the horses, peaceful and unsuspecting, walk around eating the fresh, savory grass. We had finished the work in

46

the stable hurriedly and in almost total silence. Not even Aron's little affectionate snatching in search for treats had put me in a better mood. Usually the mere sight of my horse would make me happy, but right now I felt there was no room for joy in me at all.

The other fires had been scary, but kind of harmless in a way, since nobody had been hurt. This one was different. Not only had the beautiful, red stable building at the riding school been transformed into a smoky, stinky pile of debris, but the horses, the poor innocent horses and ponies had been frightened and hurt, two of them seriously. All because of one person's evil... or madness? It didn't matter what the reason was, as long as he was caught soon. But if the police didn't find any clues this time either, that wasn't very likely to happen. Then he would be able to keep setting fires... and some night he might come here, to our stable...

"No, I refuse to think about it," I said out loud and gave a start. I had been so absorbed by my own thoughts I wasn't aware that I was saying it aloud before I heard my own voice.

"Yeah, it's just too frightening," consented Anna. "Just the thought of something happening to Quatana or Niobe and the other foals..."

She didn't say more, and we were quiet for a while.

Then Rachel suddenly said: "No, this isn't helping a bit. The more I think, the more scared and depressed I get. Let's find something constructive to do. We could teach Anna to groom a horse, for instance."

A while later, we had Quatana tethered outdoors, and Rachel and I were showing Anna how to use the sponge, the different grooming brushes and the hoof pick.

"Phew, this sure is hard work," said Anna after a while, wiping sweat from her forehead. "Oh, no," she suddenly exclaimed, pointing. "There's that incurable troublemaker again!"

Sure enough, Boris was approaching us in his usual happy and playful way. At the sight of Quatana, he started wagging his tail in pure delight. It was obvious what he had in mind, but this time Rachel was too fast for him. Quick as a panther, she descended on him and lifted him up. Boris whimpered, offended. This was not according to his plan. I had to laugh for the first time that day, because he looked so funny, kicking about and wriggling in Rachel's arms. Finally he realized that she was not going to let him go, so he started licking her face instead.

"Hey, cut it out, you little rascal. I've already washed my face today!" said Rachel, laughing. "Since you're so crazy about horses, you can play that you're a horse yourself for a while," she continued, carrying him resolutely to the stable and shutting him into one of the empty stalls.

"There, that'll keep him out of trouble!" she said triumphantly as she returned. "Now he can't pose a threat to the horses for a while."

The word threat brought back something I had dreamt last night; something about the wrong person on the wrong phone. No, wait... it was something about...

I didn't get any further, because Dad came running out of the house shouting, "Good news, everybody! We can sleep safely again! They caught that pyromaniac, or rather pyromaniacs, because there were actually two of them!"

Chapter 11

The relief was still bubbling inside me a little later when Rachel and I were riding side by side down the road after waving goodbye to Anna. She was going to have a riding lesson with Mom. The nightmare was over. We could sleep soundly again, without fear of something happening to the horses. Only the problem with Roy remained, but that was minor compared to arson, I thought. And who knows, maybe Dad had scared Roy off from contacting us anymore.

Again there was a memory trying to surface from the back of my mind. There was something wrong with that last phone call... but no matter how hard I tried, I couldn't think of what it was. I gave up, and my thoughts went instead to what Dad had said about the pyromaniacs. They had been exposed by a coincidence. Mr. Bergman, one of the teachers at the middle school, had been on his way home from a party right before the fire had started. He had seen the two on the road leading past the riding school, and had recognized them as former students. When he heard about the fire, he'd called the police and reported what he had seen, resulting in the arrest of the two. Dad had told us who they were too, because their names got out and were known all over town in no time. I actually knew one of them a little. His name was Eric, and he was a few years older than I, a sophomore in high school. He had always seemed like a nice and normal guy to me, so it was hard to imagine him doing such an awful thing. His brother, Tom, was the other one. He was twenty-two and unemployed. I knew that he had been involved in some minor crimes before.

"Not only had Mr. Bergman seen them," Dad had said. "But they'd done similar things before, so there's not much doubt that they're the guilty ones. Even though it was long ago, they've apparently had the urge since then, and now something made them start it again."

"What do you mean?" I asked, confused. "We haven't had any cases of arson in town before, have we?"

Dad had learned that the two boys, at the ages of six and ten, had tried to set fire to Randall Hansen's barn. Mr. Hansen had caught them red-handed and chased them away with a stick. Afterwards they had set fire to the woodshed back on their own ranch, but the fire had been discovered in time and put out before any major harm was done.

I was so preoccupied with my own thoughts that I hadn't even noticed where we were riding. Now I saw that we were approaching the public trail. I'd better pay attention when I get there, I thought. No point in giving some potential jogger or hiker a reason to complain by riding them down. But before we got there, I had to do an absolutely necessary errand behind the closest rock first. I guess I shouldn't have had so much juice before we left.

"I just have to make a quick stop in between the bushes," I told Rachel. "You go on ahead, and I'll catch up."

Rachel did as I said. In a hurry, I tethered Aron to a tree and gave him strict instructions to stay put. When I came back and got up in the saddle again, I heard angry yelling from the public trail.

"Oh, no!" I thought. "What happened? Did Rachel ride into a group of angry runners?"

When I got close enough to see what the commotion was, however, there was only one person besides Rachel. He was wearing a brown jacket, and had a cap pulled way down on his forehead. His dark beard was bristled, and with black sunglasses on he looked rather dubious. There was something familiar about him, but I couldn't remember where I'd seen him before. He pointed at a sign, wailing his arms about, while yelling something or other. I was curious as I rode closer, but before I reached them, the man ran into the woods and vanished.

Rachel was left sitting on Baggi, looking confused.

"Who on earth was that?" I asked.

"He said he was the forest ranger," said Rachel. "I was just riding along peacefully when I came around the bend here and saw him in between the trees over there. For a second I thought it was Roy, so I got startled and screamed. Of course, when he turned around I saw that it was a grown man, though I couldn't see his face properly because of all that beard and his cap being pulled so far down. At first it looked like he was going to turn and go, but suddenly he jumped out on the trail and started yelling at me and telling me off for riding in a place where riding isn't permitted."

She pointed at the sign, and I gaped in surprise.

"That sign has never been there before!" I said. "I can't believe it – that is so unfair!" I felt my anger rising. "Why should all the best trails be off-limits to horseback riders?"

I knew the city council had discussed the issue several times, but I hadn't expected them to suddenly put up a sign just like that.

"Regardless, it was hardly necessary for the ranger to behave so rudely," said Rachel. "If the sign was just posted, he couldn't expect me to know about it. Couldn't he have just simply told me that from now on we're not permitted to ride here?"

I was fuming with rage as we turned the horses around and rode back the same way we had come. As soon as I got into the farmyard, I called on Dad and told him what had happened. Dad got angry too when he heard how Rachel had been treated. He wasn't aware that any prohibition against horseback riding on the public trail has been determined either. "I'm going to call the city and complain right away, while I'm still irritated," he said and went into the house.

Rachel and I unsaddled the horses while he was gone. When he came back out, he had a confused expression on his face. "I don't understand this," he said. "It's apparently correct that the city council passed a new regulation which prohibits riding on that trail," he said. "But it's not certain that the decision will stand, because they've already had so many protests that they might have to reconsider it."

"Then what is it that you don't understand?" I wanted to know. "Of course people will protest a decision like that. Can't we submit a protest too?"

"Oh yes, we will," said Dad. "But that's not what I was referring to. I was thinking about this so-called ranger who yelled at Rachel."

Rachel looked questioningly at him. " Why are you saying the so-called ranger?"

"Because whoever it was, he was definitely not the ranger."

"How do you know?" I asked, curious.

"Because the ranger is at home in bed with a broken leg, and they haven't gotten a substitute for him yet," said Dad before he went into the stable.

Rachel and I looked at each other. What was going on here?

"I think..." started Rachel, but she was interrupted by Dad's voice from inside the stable. "Who locked up this poor dog in here, without food and water?" he shouted in an angry voice.

Boris! We had totally forgotten about him, and so had Mom and Anna.

Boris's tail was straight as a line as he ran past us with an offended look. He didn't even pay attention to Aron and Baggi, but just headed straight for home as fast as his legs could carry him. Poor little Boris! We hadn't intended for him to be locked up that long.

"Maybe he's had enough of stables and horses for a while now," said Rachel hopefully, as we watched him go.

I shook my head. "I wouldn't count on it," I said. "Boris isn't that easily discouraged. You just wait and see, he'll be back soon, with renewed strength!"

Chapter 12

When I turned in that night, I lay in bed thinking how good it felt not to be worrying about the arsonist anymore. Tonight my dad could sleep peacefully in his own bed again. And we'd been told that the ponies at the riding school would be well soon. That was really good news. I wondered what had made Eric and Tom do what they did. I still had a hard time believing it.

And then there was that fake ranger. I didn't understand that either. What was the point in pretending to be the ranger? Suddenly I remembered what Rachel had said. The man had been standing in between the trees and had been about to run away when he saw her. Maybe he pretended to be the ranger just because it was the best thing he could come up with on the spur of the moment? But I still didn't understand why he needed to explain what he was doing there. The area was open to all, well, except for horseback riders that is, I remembered angrily. I swear, I was not just going to send one protest to the city. I was going to drown them in protests... I'd write tons of them... big piles...

I elbowed my way through piles and piles of paper in search of the phone. It rang and rang, and I had to find it, because otherwise I would never be able to convince the city council to close the public trail to runners so that we horseback riders could have it to ourselves. There... I found the phone, but it wasn't a phone, it was an ambulance. That's good; then the ponies could get to the hospital. I watched the ambulance drive away with four ponies standing on the roof. Strange how they were able to hold on... and strange how the sound of the sirens was getting louder, even though the ambulance was driving away. I think the car had started burning, because I was smelling smoke...

"Eva, wake up! The smoke alarms are going off! The stable is burning!"

Funny how real a dream can seem, I thought, pulling the blanket over me. Then I came to. This was not a dream. The shock made me totter as I jumped out of bed and, hurrying, pulled on some jeans and a t-shirt. Then I bolted out of the room, crashing into Rachel who was also heading for the stairs. We fell over in a tangle of arms and legs. I registered vaguely that Anna rushed past us, without even noticing us lying there. We got back on our feet and scrambled down the stairs and out of the house.

My heart was beating so hard I felt like I was choking, and my ears were buzzing. Oh please, let us not be too late! Please, please,... I repeated to myself.

"The fire is in the hayloft!" I heard Dad roaring. "I've already called for the fire truck. Quick! Let's get the horses out!"

Mom had uncoiled the garden hose and had opened the faucet all the way. "Anna, come with me!" she shouted and raced up the barn ramp toward the hayloft with Anna right behind her. "Here, stay in the doorway and direct the jet of water toward the flames, she said handing the hose to Anna." "Do *not* go further in than the doorway; it's too dangerous! Just stand here and douse the flames as well as you can. Do you understand?"

I didn't hear what Anna answered because I was headed for the door into the stable as fast as my legs could carry me. From the inside I could hear frightened neighs. The horses were starting to panic, and so was I, but with great effort I managed to pull myself together. The horses needed me now. They needed all the help they could get. I had to stay calm and keep a cool head.

"Start with the stalls farthest in!" yelled Dad. "If the horses resist, throw a sweater or blanket over their heads so they can't see. That'll make it easier to get them out."

I felt the smoke get thicker as the seconds ticked by. Where was the fire truck? Weren't they coming soon? Oh yes, I could hear the sirens in the distance, but they were approaching very slowly, I thought, way too slowly!

The haste with which we needed to get the horses out made me fumble and be clumsy, and it took me twice as long as usual to get the stall doors open. Luckily the horses came with me without too much resistance, even though they were thrashing their heads about and were obviously frightened. Finally only Pinczow was left. But he refused blankly to cooperate. The temperamental young stallion was beside himself with fear. Dad tried to grab Pinczow's bridle, but had to back up several times before he succeeded. That didn't mean the problems were over, though. Pinczow reared up and was completely wild. Dad had to use all his *might* to pull him down and toward the door. Then finally they were in the doorway, just as the fire engine and other cars came howling up the driveway and rounded on the building. The piercing sound of the sirens was too much for Pinczow. He completely panicked. With a sudden and forceful motion he threw himself around, causing Dad to lose his grip and get flung backward into the wall. Pinczow took off in a wild gallop. At first he headed for the gate, but Rachel was standing there screaming and waving her arms at him, so he turned and ran toward the outfield instead, where we had put the other horses. The gate was still open. Rachel ran over and slammed it shut as soon as Pinczow was inside. There was nothing we could do to stop him now. He just had to run his panic off.

I watched as the slender, elegant horse ran off at unbelievable speed, and felt the relief flow through me. Regardless of what happened to the barn and stable, at least the horses were safe. Nothing was more important than that.

Then I turned toward the building and saw Dad lying motionless by the wall where he had fallen. Mom was kneeling down beside him. For a moment it felt as if the whole world had stopped and was standing still, like when you push the pause button in the middle of a video. I wanted to run over to my dad, but couldn't move. He wasn't... what if he was...

Rachel came running past me, and broke the paralyzing feeling inside me. I ran after her over to Mom and Dad.

Mom looked up when she heard us coming. "Go and call for an ambulance!" she said sharply. "Dad is unconscious. Hurry!"

Waiting for the ambulance to arrive was one of the worst experiences of my life. Much worse than waiting for the fire engine, because then at least there was something we could do.

Anna came running and told us that the fire had been put out, but I barely heard what she said. All my thoughts were on Dad now. Please wake up, please... I repeated inside myself over and over again. I'm not sure, but I may have said it out loud too. The whole thing started to seem like a horrible dream.

I can't describe the relief I felt when I heard the sirens at the same time Dad moved. The paramedics worked quickly and efficiently. They placed some kind of a collar around Dad's neck in case he had hurt his neck vertebrae when he fell, and then they carefully moved him onto a stretcher and carried him into the ambulance.

"Most likely a bad concussion," was all they said to us before they drove away with him.

Mom went with them in the ambulance. "I'll call as soon as I know something," she said before they closed the doors.

Rachel, Anna and I stood there, quiet and bewildered, watching as the blinking blue lights disappeared in the distance.

Chapter 13

We were having a cup of tea in the kitchen when Mom finally called. The fire fighters had gone, and the police were searching the grounds around the building, while curious neighbors who had shown up to offer their help were watching and commenting on their work. Eventually the police asked them to go home. Rachel had spoken with the police officers while Anna and I made an inspection round in the outfield to check on the horses. They seemed to have calmed down and were doing okay as far as we could tell. I had a hard time concentrating on what I was doing, because I kept thinking about Dad and what might happen to him.

When the phone rang I was in such a hurry to pick up that I almost made the whole phone fall on the floor.

"He's going to be alright and will have a full recovery!" I heard Mom's voice say, and with that I sank to the floor with a feeling of overwhelming relief.

"Eva?" said Rachel, shocked. She thought at first that it had been bad news and that I'd fainted, but then she looked at my face and understood.

I talked to Mom for a while, and then I hung up and told the others that Dad had regained consciousness. He did have a *powerful* concussion and would have to stay in the hospital for a few days, but the doctors had said he would eventually recover fully. He just had to take it easy for a few weeks.

"Well, then your mom will have to tie him down," giggled Anna. "I can't imagine your dad staying still for more than ten seconds at a time."

I started giggling too, and before we knew it, we were laughing hysterically, all three of us.

"I think I'm gonna die," sighed Rachel, holding her belly, "and I don't even know what's so funny!"

That made us launch right into another fit of laughter. At last we were just lying around on the floor, totally exhausted. I couldn't understand what we had laughed so hard about either, but I figured it might have been some kind of a reaction to all the drama we'd been through that night.

"You know what?" I said. "I completely forgot to tell Mom that the police are here."

At the same instant, the phone rang again. I sat up and answered.

"It must have been telepathy," I said when I heard my mom's voice. "We were just talking about you."

"I had to call again," said Mom. "It's unbelievable, but I totally forgot to ask if the fire is out. To be honest, I'd pretty much forgotten all about the fire because of your dad. I can tell you, I haven't been so scared in my whole life! I think I might have heard Anna say something about the fire being put out, but I wasn't at all sure. My head was spinning a little at that point, to put it mildly."

I told Mom that the fire was out, and that the damages were not too bad. They were mostly smoke damages, actually. The firemen had praised Anna for her nice job at keeping the flames in check. That had most likely saved the building from total ruin, they said.

"I can't really take credit for that," said Anna when I hung up again. "It was your mom's quick thinking to roll out the garden hose. I only did what she told me to do."

"You should have a medal, both of you," said Rachel, yawning. "How did your mom react when you told her the police were here?" she asked me.

"She said it's quite normal after a fire. The police always have to look for the cause of the fire."

"You don't think the fire was deliberate, do you?" asked Anna, horrified.

Rachel shook her head. "The arsonists are in jail," she said. "I can't image there being more than two pyromaniacs in the area. That is, if..."

She stopped suddenly, and I looked searchingly at her.

"If what?" I said.

"Nothing," she said dismissively, but I refused to leave it at that, and finally she told me that she had gotten the idea that maybe Roy could be behind this.

"But that doesn't make any sense," I said. "Why would he have done something like this? One thing is to bug you with unwanted phone calls and letters, but this wouldn't have hurt you personally! It would mostly have hurt Mom, Dad and me, as it was our stable and our horses."

"I know that," said Rachel. "That's why I didn't want to say anything. When I think about it more, it sounds stupid."

But she didn't sound too convincing, as if she wasn't quite convinced herself. I shuddered a little, because what if she was right? If Roy didn't know that the arsonist had been caught, he may have assumed that this fire would be blamed on the same person. No, it simply couldn't be true. The fire at our place must have just been an accident and nothing else, I said to myself firmly, while brushing aside the thought that an accidental fire occuring right now would be quite a coincidence.

"I'm sure the police will find that the fire started due to some fault in the electrical system or something like that," I said out loud. "Right now I just want to go to bed and not think of fires and other scary things anymore, just so you know. Good night!"

"Good morning, you mean!" said Anna, but this time nobody was laughing. We just dragged ourselves upstairs and went straight to bed. I didn't want to admit it to myself even, but deep down I was really, really glad that the police were still there, on our property.

Chapter 14

We had slept a few hours and were up and about when Mom came back from the hospital. She looked tired and drained, and no wonder. Rachel, Anna and I didn't look all that perky either, but at least we had slept a while. Dad was feeling nauseated and dizzy, Mom told us, but otherwise he was doing fine. She would be going back to the hospital later in the day.

Mom talked to the police, who were still working on their investigation when she got home. Rachel had also been outside trying to get something out of them, but all she had achieved was a request to leave them alone.

"Do they know anything about the cause of the fire?" I asked anxiously.

Mom nodded. "You won't believe this," she said with a gloomy air. "But they are quite sure that this fire was also arson!"

I felt a sinking feeling in my stomach when she said it, though I wasn't actually surprised. Deep down I had felt there had to be a connection, even though I had tried to tell myself that it wasn't possible.

When Rachel, Anna and I went to the pastures later in the day to check if the horses had water and were doing fine, we knew a lot more, and yet our confusion was greater than before.

The police, who apparently had yet another arsonist to hunt down, had contacted Mr. Bergman, the teacher who had called about Eric and Tom. They wanted Mr. Bergman to come down to the station to confirm what he had told them on the phone and sign a witness statement, or something like that.

But when the police called his house, they only got a voice mail message stating that Mr. Bergman was on vacation. Not a very smart message to leave, by the way, considering the risk of burglary. The police managed to track Mr. Bergman down, though. He was staying with some relatives. Their question took him by complete surprise, however, because as it turned out, he had not made any call to the police at all. He'd left for his vacation right after school was out, and hadn't been near the riding school at the time when he had supposedly seen Eric and Tom there.

This meant that someone else had misused his name in order to throw suspicion on two completely innocent people.

"But how could the police have been fooled so easily?" asked Anna in disbelief, as she was walking around Quatana for the umpteenth time, inspecting her from top to bottom. Quatana was grazing peacefully and contentedly, and didn't look like she had a care in the world, but Anna seemed to think that some hidden injury would miraculously pop up on the horse's body as soon as she turned her back.

Rachel grabbed Anna's arm. "Please stop, you're making me dizzy, the way you're rotating around that poor horse," she said. "Quatana is just fine, you know. She wouldn't be walking around eating so greedily if she were hurting."

Anna laughed, slightly embarrassed. Then she sat down over by the fence and repeated her question. "I don't understand it," she added. "Can just anybody call the police and say a name, and be trusted just like that? In that case we could all risk being arrested!"

"I think they ask for date of birth and phone number," said Rachel. "So whoever did this must know both. The phone number isn't hard to find; you can just look it up in the directory. But his date of birth wouldn't be that easy to get a hold of, would it?"

"Well, in the case of Mr. Bergman, it would be the simplest thing in the world," I said. "He just turned fifty a few weeks ago, and there was an article about him in the local newspaper on his birthday. But whoever pretended to be him must have sounded quite convincing, because otherwise the police would have discovered the error pretty quickly, I think."

"Even if there had been no fire here last night, they would have found out some time today regardless," said Rachel. "They couldn't keep Eric and Tom in custody without Mr. Bergman coming in to give a proper statement in person."

"But then what's the point of going to all that trouble to get two innocent people arrested?" I said, thinking out loud. "It doesn't make any sense, especially since the real arsonist had apparently planned to continue setting fires. Then the truth would come out pretty quickly anyway."

"Maybe he just needed some time," said Rachel thoughtfully.

"Time? What do you mean?" I stared incomprehensibly at her.

"Of course!" Anna burst out. "That's the only thing that makes sense!"

"Am I stupid, or what?" I said, looking from one to the other. "I have no idea what you guys are talking about!"

"What would have happened if those two hadn't been arrested yesterday?" asked Rachel.

"Happened?" I still didn't understand what she was getting at.

"Yes, what would have happened at the stable here last night, if the two suspects hadn't been taken into custody?"

Finally I saw the light. "Of course!" I said. "Dad would have been keeping watch, and so would a lot of other ranch owners.

"Especially the ones who own horses," said Anna. "Have you noticed that all the places that the arsonist has targeted have horses?"

I hadn't thought about that before, but Anna was right. Maybe the arsonist was a person who hated horses? If so, who could that be? I thought really hard. Nobody I knew of fit that description, that is, except...

My thoughts were interrupted by Rachel's voice.

"Since the arsonists were supposedly behind bars, the real arsonist had free reign to strike again," she said. "Is it possible that the fire here was supposed to be the big climax? Because now that everybody knows that Eric and Tom are innocent, people will be on their guard more than ever. It won't be so easy to do it again after this."

"In that case he must be quite disappointed right now, because it

62

didn't exactly turn into a big devastating fire," said Anna. "Maybe he didn't know that you had lots of smoke alarms all through the building."

"Do you think he might come back?" I asked, afraid. "He would be insane to do that. But then, he probably is insane," said Rachel. "You have to be pretty screwed up in the head to do something like this in the first place. Dangerously screwed up."

A chill crept up my spine at the thought of this insane, evil person coming back to finish what he had started. And next time he might succeed...

Chapter 15

"I'm leaving now!" yelled Mom. "I assume you guys can take care of yourselves. Just look in on the horses sometime this evening. I'll be home before ten."

"Give my best to Dad for me," I said.

"From us too!" yelled Rachel and Anna after her. "And tell him he'd better practice a little more before he tries some rodeo stunt like that again," Rachel added.

"I will," laughed Mom and went out the door.

I looked at the time. It was only 2:30. "How about giving Anna a riding lesson for a while?" I suggested. "It'll give us something to do."

"Good idea," said Rachel. "Then we can go for a ride afterward."

"I'll use the bike and come too," said Anna. "I'm not hurting as much anymore."

"Practice is rough but makes your behind tough," laughed Rachel as she went into the stable to get the saddle and bridle for Quatana. The smell was really bad in there from the smoke and soot. We weren't allowed to start cleaning it up or making repairs before the claims examiner from the insurance company had been out to look at the damages. I hoped he would come soon, because it was very unpleasant to have the stable and hayloft in that shape.

"Phew, I do look forward to riding on a horse myself," shouted Anna, as she was peddling really hard behind us. "There you are, just enjoying the ride, while the horses and I have to work like a... like a..."

"Horse?" I suggested, laughing teasingly. My mood had improved considerably during our ride. It helped to get away for a while, in the company of good friends and the world's most wonderful horse. It's funny that I was now thinking of Anna as a good friend, while I had initially thought I wouldn't be able to stand her at all when I heard she was coming. Not everything turns out the way you expect it to, I philosophized, as I ruffled Aron's mane.

Rachel hadn't mentioned Roy all day, but I don't think she felt completely safe from him yet, because she suggested we ride in the fields instead of in the woods.

"But how can I bike there?" objected Anna.

She had a point, so we ended up riding along the road instead. There wasn't much traffic, and plenty of gravel on the side of the road, so the horses didn't have to walk on the asphalt.

"It really irritates me that we're not allowed to use the public trail anymore," I said. "That trail is good for biking as well."

Mentioning the public trail made me think about that fake ranger who had behaved so threateningly toward Rachel. We still didn't know who he was, or why he behaved the way he did. Could he have been the same person we had seen the other times in the woods, and if so, did he have something to do with the fires? Was that why he was sneaking around in the woods, not wanting to be seen?

No, it was no use sitting there wondering about those things, because I didn't get any answers from it, only more confusion. I shook off the thoughts that were bothering me and concentrated instead on my riding. I thought I'd better not sit and daydream when there could be cars coming by any minute.

"We could make a loop over to the Hansen house," I suggested. "Then we have a dirt road the whole way, and no cars at all."

As we approached the house, Anna suddenly said, "I thought I saw somebody in one of the windows."

I stared at the house, but couldn't see anything unusual. We rode around the house and checked doors and windows, but nothing suggested that anybody was there.

"It was probably the light that played a trick on you, just like it did when Eva and I rode past here the other day," said Rachel.

But when we rode away from the house, I got that same icky feeling as last time, that someone was watching me.

Chapter 16

"We've been forgetting to pick up the mail," I said, as we were taking the saddles off Aron and Baggi a little later.

"I'll go and get it," said Anna. "It's probably just a bunch of junk mail as usual."

"You can just dump it directly into the recycling bin," I told Anna when she came back with an armfull of colorful brochures and ads. "Right now I doubt Mom will be very interested in which store has peas or chicken on sale."

"There's a letter here too," said Anna as she held up a grayish-white envelope.

"Let me see," said Rachel, snapping the envelope out of Anna's hand. Her own hands were shaking as she turned the envelope, which didn't have any stamp on it. As far as I could see, the envelope was identical to the one Rachel had found on the front porch a few days ago.

Nothing was written on the outside of the envelope. Rachel ripped it open and unfolded the sheet inside. I felt my heart skip a beat when I read the words written on it: Next time I'll succeed! Nobody does wrong against me unpunished!

"Roy! He's been here again! He's still in this neighborhood! How stupid I've been, to not understand the connection before! But this is enough! I will not be terrorized anymore!" Rachel dropped the sheet of paper on the ground and started saddling up Baggi rapidly and determinedly.

I just stood there looking at her. I didn't understand her reaction. Until now, Rachel had seemed scared every time the topic of Roy came up. Suddenly she was just furious. And where in the world was she going?

I was so confused by this new development that I couldn't bring myself to say or do anything. And then Rachel swung herself into the saddle on Baggi. That's when I got my wits about me again.

"What are you doing?" I asked. "You can't just ride out looking for Roy all by yourself!"

"I don't have to look for him; I know where he is!" said Rachel. "It's so obvious. I can't believe I didn't see it before! How could I have been so blind? But now I see, and I've had enough of his terrorizing. I'm going to confront him, and tell him to stay away from me, if it's the last thing I do!"

"But what if he's dangerous?" I objected. "I thought you were scared of him."

"Not anymore! I'm quite sure he won't do anything to harm me. He wouldn't dare, because I'll tell him that you and everyone else in this house know where I am and that I went to talk to him."

With that she took off on Baggi's back before I could say another word.

"Rachel!" I screamed after her. "We don't know where you're going! You haven't told us where he is!"

But Rachel didn't answer. I just stood there helplessly, watching her leave. Where in the world was she going? And what did she mean, that she should have seen it before?

When it finally came to me what she had meant, I understood why she had said she had been blind. The Hansen house, of course! It was the ideal hideout for someone who didn't want to be seen. All those times I had felt as if someone was inside the house, watching me. Even so, I hadn't thought to connect it with the mysterious Roy. I had just brushed it aside as imagination. Oh yes, "blind" was a good description for me too.

Hurrying, I explained to Anna what I had been thinking. I picked up the letter while I was talking. The words on it seemed threatening and strange. Was it likely that a young boy would write something like that to a girl he was in love with? Even if he was unbalanced and sensitive?

While I was standing there looking at the letter, I suddenly remembered what had seemed so wrong about the last phone call. It had been Dad who answered the phone, not Rachel. Even so, Roy had delivered his threatening message. It didn't make sense. If he was calling to threaten Rachel, wouldn't he have asked for her, or simply hung up and tried again later, hoping that she would be the one answering?

What if it wasn't Roy who had called or written the anonymous letters at all? What if it was someone else? And what if this someone else was hiding out in the Hansen house? At least I did feel that Rachel might be right about someone hiding out over there.

I read the letter again. If it wasn't Roy who had written it, who could it be, and why? The answer came to me before I even got a chance to think about it. Who had just failed at something? The arsonist! He hadn't succeeded in burning down our stable. Suddenly the words on the sheet made perfect sense, that is, if you can call such madness sense. He had failed, but was going to try again. But what did he mean by doing wrong against him? I didn't understand that part. And I didn't have time to think about it either, because if I was right, Rachel could be in deadly danger right now. He had already shown that he didn't care whether life was lost. Animal life, perhaps, but I had no guarantee that he had any greater concern for human life.

"C'mon!" I called out to Anna, who was standing there watching me with a confused look. "This is urgent! Rachel might be at the Hansen house already! We can ride the shortcut across the fields on Aron!"

I didn't dare ride bareback with Anna on the horse with me, so I took time to saddle up Aron really fast.

"Come on," I said to Anna, "jump up behind me and hold on! I can't explain right now, but I think Rachel could be in serious danger!"

Anna did as I said, without hesitation or questions.

Aron cast a surprised glance back at Anna and me, as if he wondered if we were in our right mind. He seemed to think, hadn't we just been on a ride? Had I forgotten already?

But when we got out in the field, he was more than willing to stretch out, even if he did have an extra burden on his back. Anna clung to me as tightly as she could.

68

I glanced quickly at my watch. Rachel had about a fifteen-minute head start on us. And as furious as she had been when she took off, she had probably stormed right into the house to tell Roy off. The thought of something really bad happening to Rachel made my stomach tie up in knots.

Never had such a short ride seemed so long! But finally we got to the little clearing that marked the old border between our property and the Hansen ranch. I noticed that dark clouds were gathering above the treetops, and had a brief thought that we might get some rain tonight. Then I realized that it wasn't clouds, but thick, grayish black smoke that was rising into the sky.

"There's a fire!" I shouted to Anna.

I can't describe the shock of seeing the Hansen house in flames. The entire house was engulfed in the flames, which were extending out the windows and across the roof.

"Rachel might be in there!" I screamed in total panic.

Anna got so shocked, she forgot to hold on to me, and before I knew what was happening, I was alone in the saddle. I saw Anna behind me, sitting in the grass staring trance-like at the burning house. She didn't even seem to have noticed that she had fallen off the horse. I stopped Aron and looked frantically around for something to tether him to. Then I saw Baggi. He was tethered to a tree a short distance away. Hurriedly I led Aron over there and tethered him to the tree next to him. My hands trembled so much I could barely do it. The thought of Rachel being trapped inside the house made my insides turn.

In the distance I could hear the sound of sirens. Someone in the vicinity must have discovered the fire and called, but the fire engine would be too late, way too late, I thought desperately.

"Look! She's over there!" screamed Anna suddenly.

I turned away from Aron and saw what Anna was pointing at. Rachel was standing in front of the burning house, with the flames like a ghastly light show behind her back. Her eyes were staring transfixed into the air, and it didn't look like she had seen us. It didn't look like she saw anything at all.

The relief of seeing her standing safely on the outside made me shake like a leaf. My knees were knocking against each other, and I could barely stay on my feet as I walked unsteadily toward the house.

"Rachel!" I tried to yell, but my voice was just a hoarse quack and she didn't hear me. At least she didn't respond.

"Rachel!" roared Anna, and this time she jumped and looked toward us. Seconds later we were embracing each other, all three of us.

"I thought you were dead," I gasped into Rachel's hair. It reeked of smoke.

"The heroine never dies," said Rachel with a quivering laugh. Then she sank to the ground. "He tried to kill me," she said and started crying. "Roy was going to kill me!"

"It wasn't Roy," I started, but I don't think she heard me. I sat down next to her and put my arm around her shoulders. Explanations could wait until later. Anna sat down on the other side of Rachel, who cried as her whole body shook. We let her cry in peace. And we sat like that for quite a while.

Chapter 17

"Hey, move it, I want a window seat too," I told Anna, and elbowed my way in between her and Rachel.

It was late that same evening, and as tired as we all were, we were not about to miss out on what would most likely happen that night. We had been pleading with Mom to let us hide in the stable, but she wouldn't hear of it.

"I do believe you're out of your minds! Wasn't it bad enough that Rachel risked her life because of thoughtlessness?" she had said, shaking her head in exasperation. "What I'd really like to do is to send you away, all three of you, until this insane, murderous guy is safely behind bars. You won't even go anywhere near the stable tonight, is that clear?"

Finally she had agreed to let us sit up in the master bedroom, which had a view of the stable. She herself went to bed on the couch in the living room. "I won't be able to sleep anyway, before that madman is caught," she said.

"I can't see the police anywhere," complained Anna as she made room for me. "What if they're not there?"

"Of course they are," said Rachel. "Don't you think they'd like to catch the arsonist in the act?"

"I don't think we should lean so far forward, I said." "Even if we don't have any light on in the room, he might be able to see us if we have our noses pressed against the window. Remember we promised Mom to keep quiet and not ruin anything for the police."

I thought about what had happened earlier that day, and had to touch Rachel to kind of assure myself that she really was there, safe and sound.

It felt as if we had been spending half the day being interrogated by the police. What Rachel had experienced was like right out of a horror movie.

She had arrived at the Hansen house, still fuming mad, and had tethered Baggi at a good distance from the house. Then she marched up to the house, banged on the door and shouted: "I know you're in there, Roy! I want to talk to you!"

Nobody had answered, even though Rachel could hear someone moving in there. The door was unlocked, so she had walked inside. When inside, she didn't see any sign of Roy. Nor was there any indication that somebody had been hiding out downstairs, but then she heard a door being shut. The sound came from upstairs.

And Rachel, who was still too furious to think clearly, had been foolhardy enough to go upstairs.

"One of the doors on the second floor was cracked," she said. "I called out for Roy and peeked inside. At that moment somebody pushed me from behind, making me stumble into the room. Before I managed to turn around, the door was slammed shut, and I heard the door being locked from the outside. I ran over and banged on the door, yelling at Roy that this was not funny. That he was a cowardly jerk who could terrorize people by phone, but when it came down to it, was not brave enough to talk to me face-to-face."

The person she assumed to be Roy hadn't answered. All she heard when she finally gave up yelling and banging on the door was somebody rummaging around with something downstairs. She heard clattering and banging and wondered what he was doing. "I was still more angry than afraid," Rachel said. "But as I gradually started realizing that he didn't intend to let me out, I started getting scared. And then I suddenly saw how stupid it had been to go there alone."

"Stupid is only the first name," I said. "You almost scared Anna and me to death. Never do something like that again, you hear?"

"Don't worry." Rachel shuddered. "When I think about how it could have ended if it hadn't been for that downspout..."

Rachel had been looking around for a way out of the room when she heard footsteps on the stairs. For a moment she thought

Roy had changed his mind and come to let her out. But she only heard some banging noises and the sound of splashing through the door.

"I didn't understand what he was doing until the smell of gasoline reached me through the cracks. Then I panicked. I screamed and yelled for him to let me out, and that he couldn't seriously want to kill me! But he didn't answer me at all. He just went back down the stairs. A moment later I could hear the crackling of fire, which turned into a roar as the flames flared up along the stairs and hall where he had poured out the gasoline."

"I can't believe you managed to keep a cool head," said Anna.

"Oh, I didn't." Rachel shuddered again. "All I could think was that the stairs were closed and that I had to get out the window somehow. I meant to jump, I think, but when I flung the window open, I discovered the downspout nearby. I have no memory of how I managed to get over to it and climb down, but suddenly I was standing on the ground outside the house. Then I kind of froze, unable to move anymore. I was just standing there, with a single thought churning in my head, that Roy meant to kill me! Roy wanted to kill me! And then you guys came." Rachel hadn't seen the arsonist run from the house, but he must have because there had been no signs of human remains in the debris. After Rachel told the police what had happened, I also told them what I had found out. They seemed pretty skeptical at first, but started taking me seriously after a while. And they managed, surprisingly fast, to find a common motive for all the fires. With a little more time, I would probably have seen it too, now that I know who the guilty one was. I just couldn't believe why we hadn't seen it before. At least Dad should have figured it out, I thought.

"There's something moving over there!" said Anna, interrupting my thoughts.

I looked through the window in the direction she was pointing, but didn't see anything.

"Nah, I guess it was nothing," said Anna disappointed.

We waited quite a while longer, but nothing happened. I was

starting to get sleepy, but I definitely didn't want to go to sleep now. So I got up and walked to the door. "I'm thirsty," I said. "I'll go down to the kitchen and get some water. Anyone else want some?"

Anna and Rachel shook their heads, and I fumbled my way down the dark stairs and into the kitchen. Don't turn on any lights now, I reminded myself.

I jumped as the door to the living room was opened, but it was just Mom peeking in. "Oh, it's just you," she said, relieved. "I heard some noises in here, so I decided I'd better check what it was."

"I just need some water," I said. "It's so..."

"Hush!" hissed Mom. "What was that?"

I stood completely still and listened. Then I heard it too, a barely audible, scraping sound, and then a thump.

"There's somebody outside the kitchen door!" I whispered into Mom's ear.

She nodded, then walked stealthily across the room and quietly opened a cabinet door. I wondered what she was up to, but then I heard the scraping sound again and concentrated on the door instead. My heart was pounding like a hammer in my chest.

The arsonist was outside. Why I was so sure it was him, I have no idea. I just knew it without a doubt. And the police were on the other side of the house somewhere, watching the stable! Some way or another he had managed to sneak up to the house unseen. We had been so sure that he would come back to make another attempt at burning down our barn with the stable and everything. It hadn't occurred to us that he might go for the house instead.

What I really wanted to do was fling the window open and scream for help, but then he might get away.

When Mom put a hand on my shoulder I got so startled I almost screamed anyway.

"Let's show him who he's up against," my mom whispered in my ear. "Go to the door, fling it open, and whatever you do, get out of the way!"

My legs were trembling, but I did as she said, and flung the

74

door open. But when I saw the distorted, insane expression on Randall Hansen's face, I couldn't move out of the way, like Mom had told me to do. He jumped as he saw me, but then his expression turned into an evil grin as he reached out one hand to grab me. In the other hand he held a gasoline can. I wanted to pull away from his threatening hand, but felt totally unable to move an inch. Then I was pushed aside by Mom. She was running out the door with the broom raised in her hands, and started beating Randall Hansen with it, making him lose his balance and fall.

In the next moment the house was swarming with policemen who immediately restrained Randall Hansen and put him in hand-cuffs.

He roared and yelled so loudly it was probably heard miles away. "You stole my ranch! You will pay for that! You just wait, I'll be back and then I'll burn it all down! Nobody does wrong against me unpunished! Do you hear? Nobody!"

He was still screaming threats and curses when the police shoved him into a car and took him away. Anna and Rachel came running down the stairs when they heard the noise outside, and we all just stood there dumbfounded and speechless, looking after the car driving that deadly madman away. I had expected to feel relief at the fact that the arsonist was finally behind bars, but right then I wasn't able to feel anything at all, just a heavy numbness throughout my body.

"Come on, you three," said my mom firmly. "Off to bed! Now we need to sleep. Tomorrow we can talk about all that has happened."

We all walked quietly to our bedrooms with no objections, and I must have fallen asleep the moment I put my head on the pillow.

Chapter 18

The next day I felt dizzy and beat up, as if I had run a marathon or something. "I feel so stupid," said Rachel as we were sitting down by the pasture watching the horses after having eaten a late breakfast. The horses were eating juicy, green grass while flapping their tails to get rid of irritable flies.

"Why?" I said. "How were you supposed to know it was Randall Hansen setting those fires all over town? It was the rest of us who should have figured it out – especially Dad, who was at the auction."

"Imagine, that crazy lunatic setting a fire to the barn of everyone who had bid on his ranch during the auction," said Anna, shaking her head in disbelief. "It's actually kind of strange that the police didn't piece it together earlier."

"Nobody thought of it," I said. "We all just assumed that he had left and was gone for good. Now it turns out that he had left the camper with all his stuff in the woods a few miles away from here. He drove it there and parked it. Then he went back to his house. He's been staying there, upstairs, the whole time."

"Except when he was sneaking around, spying and planning where to set the next fire," said Rachel, shuddering.

"I'm sure it was him pretending to be the ranger too, that day on the trail," I said. "I thought there was something familiar about that man. If I had gotten a closer look at him, the mystery might have been solved then and there."

"That's probably why he left so fast," stated Rachel. "So you wouldn't get a chance to recognize him. He had probably meant to disappear when I showed up, too, but might have thought it would look suspicious. So he pretended to be the ranger and started yelling at me instead."

"Mom says it's likely he's been insane for a long time," I said slowly. "And then the forced auction made him lose it completely. It was his own fault that he had to give up his ranch, but in his twisted mind all the blame was transferred to those who wanted to buy the ranch. He hated all of them, but us most of all, since we were the ones who got it. That's why he was calling and leaving notes threatening us, but not the others. I imagine he enjoyed getting Tom and Eric into trouble too, because apparently he never forgave them for almost setting fire to his barn all those years ago."

"If he had written threatening notes to everyone who bid on his ranch during the auction, somebody would probably have figured out the connection much earlier," commented Anna.

"You would probably have figured it out long ago regardless, if it hadn't been for me," said Rachel, shaking her head in resignation. "That's why I said I feel so stupid. I was so sure Roy was behind the calls and the notes that I pretty much hypnotized you all into believing it too."

I looked at her. Poor Rachel, she looked so guilt-ridden. But how could she not have thought it was Roy, considering his strange behavior before she left?

We had actually confirmed that Roy didn't have anything at all to do with this. Rachel had called home and talked to her parents. Her mom had just met Roy's mom the other day, and she had mentioned that Roy was in Mexico. He had called his parents collect the day before, which would prove he was where he said he was. And he had been excited about some girl he had met on the way to Mexico.

"But even though I'm feeling really stupid for suspecting him, I'm still really relieved that it wasn't Roy who was following me," continued Rachel. "And I'm even more happy that he's met another girl that he's interested in. Then I don't have to worry about him bothering me anymore when I get home."

"Do you think Randall Hansen will be in prison for a long time?" asked Anna suddenly.

Rachel seemed happy to leave the subject of Roy. "I doubt he'll go to prison at all," she said. "Most likely he'll end up in a closed ward at some psychiatric hospital."

"Well, I don't care where they put him, as long as they don't let him out for a long time," said Anna. "But let's talk about more pleasant things. When can I go horseback riding with you guys?"

"Well, that could be really soon," smiled Rachel. "Why don't we have a riding lesson right now, and see how it goes?"

We got Quatana from the pasture and saddled her up. Anna swung herself into the saddle, a little awkward still, but without any big problems. I couldn't believe this was the same girl who had screamed hysterically when a horse came near her. If her mom could see her now, she'd probably be the one to become hysterical. Anna was sitting straight and nicely in the saddle, holding the reins in a secure grip. She'd be a fine rider as soon as she got some more practice.

"This is really fun!" said Anna excitedly as Rachel guided her through walk, trot and a short canter. Anna didn't even waver once in the saddle.

"You're almost ready to go for a ride," stated Rachel. "You just have to learn how to stop a horse who's running. Not because Quatana is easily scared or has a tendency to run, but it's safer to know what to do regardless."

Anna nodded. "I'm looking forward to it already," she said. "I could never have imagined that the day I came here. Back then I thought the horses were big, ugly, and scary. Now I think they are big, beautiful, and totally fantastic! The rest of this summer break will be really great, don't you think so too?"

While we were standing in the paddock helping Anna take off the saddle, a car drove up the driveway. Two men got out and walked over toward the barn.

"The claims examiners!" I said. "Good! Then we can start fixing the stable again, and remove every sign of Hansen's ugly ravaging. I don't want there to be anything left reminding me of that madman."

"Look on the bright side," said Anna, grinning. "Now you don't have to tear down his house."

She had a point. The firemen had actually allowed the house to burn to the ground, because they knew it was about to be demolished anyway. They had merely concentrated on preventing the fire from spreading to trees or bushes. And that was just as well, I thought.

"I agree," I said. "The sooner we remove all debris and let fresh, new grass cover up all traces of that awful animal abuser and arsonist, the better."

"Oh, darn!" said Rachel suddenly. "Do you see what I see?"

"The horses!" exclaimed Anna, "they're leaving the pasture. We must have forgotten to close the gate properly."

Rachel sprinted over there and just barely managed to close the gate right in front of Assisam. He stomped his hooves and looked very offended to have his escape route blocked this way.

I gave a sigh of relief. That crazy horse wouldn't have been easy to catch, if he'd gotten loose and taken off down the road.

The three horses who were on the loose right now were not a big deal. They wouldn't go anywhere, and we just had to lead them back to the pasture. They came walking slowly toward the paddock to say hello to Quatana. She greeted them with an excited snort.

I slowly reached my arm out to grab the bridle on Pinczow, who was closest. At the same moment a black and white whirlwind on four legs entered the paddock. Boris!

He hadn't been around since he had been so offensively locked up in the stable, but apparently he was ready to play with the horses again. Wild and excited, he ran toward Pinczow, barking frantically. Then he stopped and shook his head back and forth, trying to decide which horse to play with first.

Pinczow, however, seemed to finally have had enough of the little troublemaker who was always being such a nuisance. His ears were lying flat back as he attacked. In a powerful jump, making his body turn into an elegant arch, he threw himself at Boris, who had his back turned just then.

I held my breath. How was this going to end? Even though Boris was a real nuisance, he was also incredibly cute, and I didn't want him to get hurt.

I think some kind of sixth sense warned Boris that something bad was about to happen. As Pinczow was about right over him, Boris turned his head and saw the enormous horse body descending on him.

With a shocked yelp he threw himself away from the menacing horse, and ran to safety behind me. He stayed there, looking bewildered at Pinczow, who galloped around for a while from the excitement.

I scooped Boris up and held him, and he started licking my nose.

"You're such a crazy dog, you know that?" I said. "You have to stop this nonsense before you get seriously injured, do you hear me?"

Boris wagged his tail, and apparently thought I was praising him. I had to laugh.

"Maybe now he's finally had the lesson he needed," suggested Anna optimistically.

"I don't believe it for a moment," I laughed. "This dog is and always will be incorrigible, and I'm quite sure we have many more excitements to look forward to. Right?" I said, ruffling his fur.

"Woof!" said Boris.

Part 2:
Without Scruples

Chapter 1

"Yes, Mom, of course everything is ok. Why wouldn't it be?" I moved the phone to the other ear and rolled my eyes in a resigned expression toward Rachel, who was cleaning wet straw out of Pinczow's stall. Rachel grinned and continued working.

"It's only been two hours since you left home, you know. Where are you now, by the way, at the airport?"

I only half listened, as my mom's voice sounded like a motor in my ear. I could feel the irritation growing inside me. How old did she think I was, anyway? Five?! It was quite all right that she didn't want me to be home alone for three whole weeks while she and Dad went on their long-desired vacation to Italy. My parents were in the middle of a tiring job of replacing the siding on the house. Next they would be fixing the roof. So they needed a couple of weeks away to recharge, as my mom put it.

I didn't mind having Rachel stay with me. Since we rent out pasture to other horse owners, meaning that in the summer we have cold-blooded horses as well as small and large ponies grazing in our meadows, it would have been too much for me to take care of all the horses by myself. But Mom doesn't have to act as if I'm some helpless little kid for that reason.

Initially the plan was for Rachel to bring her horse Nupùr with her to our place, but then she decided to leave him in their own pasture for the three weeks that she would be staying with me.

I became aware of Mom's voice again. "… And you know, Eva, when I heard on the radio on the way here that there had been another burglary, I couldn't help but worry. Please make sure you lock all the doors and windows at night…"

I cut her off. "Burglary? Where?"

"I didn't hear them say where, just that the elderly lady who lived in the house had been assaulted in her own home, in broad daylight! Isn't it terrible?"

There had been a series of burglaries in the neighborhood in the last few weeks, so maybe Mom did have a good reason to be worried. But all the burglaries had happened to elderly people who lived alone, so I figured I would be outside the danger zone. I reminded my mom of this, and apparently managed to calm her fears, because she went on to talk about her vacation again, and how much she looked forward to finally getting to see Rome. I had heard all this about four hundred times already, so I just gave the standard responses in what I hoped were the appropriate places while I waited for her to finish.

When Mom had finally said her goodbyes, and I had told her to have a good trip one more time, my ear was all sweaty.

"Is your mom still worried?" asked Rachel. She had heard the whole story about the burglaries and my mom's worries the night before.

I nodded and went to get the pitchfork I had put down when my cell phone rang. "Apparently there's been another burglary, and an old lady was assaulted."

"That's scary! I sure hope the police catch the perpetrator or perpetrators soon," Rachel said as she threw a load of wet straw toward the wheelbarrow. She missed, and the fork load landed right across my shoes. "Oops! Sorry, Eva," she laughed, while I hastily pulled my shoes out of the stinking mess.

"No problem," I said. "Now at least nobody can tell I have sweaty feet."

I went into Quatana's stall and looked with adoration at the beautiful, shiny, grayish white mane of the gray filly. Although she's a full blooded Arabian, just like Aron, they couldn't look more different. Dad has always claimed that Quatana is the most perfect of all our horses. He may think so, but as far as I'm concerned, none of them can measure up to my Aron, who's now a six-year-old.

Recently though, Aron had been struggling with minor leg injuries, which made Dad decide to take him to a pasture for the entire summer. I had been under the impression that Aron would be in one of our own pastures on the farm, but since Mom and Dad were going away for several weeks, Dad wanted Aron to be under the supervision of a friend of his who had expertise in the treatment of leg injuries. The problem was that this friend lived more than an hour's drive from our farm. So I was going to have to go several weeks without getting as much as a glimpse of my precious horse. I missed him already, even though I knew he was well taken care of.

Quatana rubbed her muzzle against my arm and snorted lightly. Then she shook her head, making her mane dance. I scratched her forehead. "You're not upset, are you? I had to talk to Mom, you know."

"Do you want to go for a ride after we're done here?" Rachel asked. She was just passing Quatana's stall with a heavily-loaded wheelbarrow.

"Sure," I said. "We deserve it after having worked so hard for hours."

"Ha! I've worked hard. You've been standing around gabbing on the phone," said Rachel, as she disappeared out the door with her load. A moment later I heard a shriek and a clunk.

I ran outside. Rachel sat on the ground with the wheelbarrow on its side next to her, and hay and sawdust all over the place. She was trying to keep a black and white furball out of her face, but didn't succeed too well, as the fur ball was wild with delight, and a thick, bushy tail swept back and forth, whipping up the sawdust around her. Its long, pink tongue was licking Rachel's face and anything else it could get to.

"Boris!" I yelled in a stern voice. "Get away from Rachel, you bad dog!"

"Oh, leave him alone," laughed Rachel. "He just wanted to say hello. Imagine, he remembers me after all this time." "He attacked me as soon as I got out the door," Rachel said with a chuckle, ruffling Boris's fur. He rolled over on his back, so Rachel could

85

scratch his tummy. The shaggy tail was still wagging like crazy. "It's only been a year, but I'd totally forgotten how high he can jump."

As Rachel had just learned, Boris's owner, Mr. Anderson, had lost his wife just six months ago. Since Mr. Anderson's not very agile anymore, Boris stops by more and more frequently to say hello, and maybe sneak a little treat around dinnertime. Boris has gotten fond of my Dad's hamburgers, and will do anything to get a bite of one when he gets a whiff of his favorite food from the kitchen.

"Maybe he thought you were a horse," I said laughingly and shook my head. "Too bad my parents have the camera with them, or I could have gotten a picture of you now."

"You wouldn't dare!" snorted Rachel. "If you did that, I would make a whole picture series of you early in the morning, trying to find your way to the bathroom!"

She had me on that one. It's no secret that I'm a little out of it right after I wake up, and I wouldn't like to be caught by a photo lens in that state. With my hair all in a big tangle, and squinting, unfocused eyes trying to find the bathroom door, I would hardly win any "Face of the Year" award. Not that I would have any other time, either. Maybe it was just as well the camera was on its way to Italy.

Rachel finally managed to free herself from Boris and start to shovel the scattered straw back into the wheelbarrow. Meanwhile, Boris saw his chance to sneak into the stable. I quickly went after him. You never know what Boris might do in there. He was standing by Quatana's stall with a look full of anticipation. He looked as if he were saying: "Just wait until you get out, and then we can have so much fun." Quatana didn't look as excited. She's never been scared of Boris, but she hates having a yapping dog running between her feet.

"C'mon Boris," I said firmly, and grabbed his collar. "It's time for you to go home." Boris wagged his tail. "I mean it! You do not get to go with us on the ride." I looked sternly at him.

Out in the farmyard I shooed him off in the direction of Mr.

Anderson's house. I couldn't believe it when he actually obeyed. The ruffled tail was wagging for as long as I could see him. He was so incredibly cute. If he just weren't so mischievous around horses! I had a feeling that it wouldn't be long before he was back, though, ready for new escapades.

Chapter 2

While Rachel and I were getting Quatana and Baggi ready for our ride a little later, Rachel said, "Imagine your parents leaving without the camera! Do you think we ought to send a message to their hotel and tell them that it's here? They might think it got lost or stolen on the way. It's an expensive camera, after all."

I shook my head. "I'm sure they'll understand that they left it behind. And they're going to call and check if we found it regardless. It serves them right if they think it's lost or stolen. They've been calling over and over again, not trusting us to remember to lock the house even. And what do they do? Leave half of their luggage behind when they go on vacation!"

Rachel and I had been quite surprised when we came inside to change into our riding clothes and found the camera in the entrance, partially buried by a heap of shoes that my mom had tried on and discarded before they left.

"Isn't it a slight exaggeration to call the camera half of the luggage?" Rachel said with a laugh. "However, you're probably right that they'll call. You know, we could just leave the message on the answering machine. Then they'll find out, even if we're not home when they call."

"Good idea!" I ran inside and recorded the message "Hi! We're a little busy right now, but if this is Mom or Dad calling, the camera is here and safe. A touch of Alzheimer's, you think?" Then I set the answering machine to answer. If anyone else called now, they wouldn't understand a thing, but oh well.

"This is wonderful!" exclaimed Rachel happily when we took off a little later, riding the horses at a walking pace on a quiet road, heading for some nice riding trails in the woods.

I nodded in agreement. Nothing beats the feeling of sitting on the strong, safe back of a horse who carries you through the terrain. The feeling of that enormous power in its body is fantastic, and you know that the sturdy kind animal which right now is walking along at a lazy pace, will launch at your signal into an explosion of power and shoot off in swift gallop.

I bent forward and patted Quatana on the neck. "You're the best, you know that?"

She nodded contentedly, as if she understood what I said and agreed completely. Well, second best after Aron, I thought to myself, but I didn't say it out loud, because I didn't want to hurt Quatana's feelings.

We were almost to the edge of the woods when we saw a lonely figure, dressed in a dark sweater and light-colored jeans, walking toward us. When he came closer I saw who it was, and said hi as we passed each other. He looked up for a moment, mumbled a short "hi" himself, and quickened his pace as he walked on.

"Well, he was charming," said Rachel sarcastically when we were out of earshot. "Who was that?"

"His name is Rob and he's in my class," I said. "He's Stephanie's twin brother. They moved here a few months ago."

"Oh yes, I remember you mentioned Stephanie," said Rachel. "You said she comes here to help with the horses in exchange for free riding. I hope she's friendlier than her brother seems to be."

"Oh, she is," I said. "She had a dentist appointment this morning, otherwise she would most likely have come on the ride with us. You'll probably see her later today. Stephanie is nice and all, but she can be a little moody sometimes. I have an impression that she might have problems at home, but she doesn't like to talk about it, so I don't ask. We end up talking mostly about horses."

While we were riding into the woods on the soft and peaceful forest trail, I told Rachel what little I knew about Stephanie and Rob, in addition to what the town gossip had told me about their family.

Stephanie's mom divorced their dad when they were little, and

Stephanie and Rob had not seen him since. That much I knew, because Stephanie had told me herself. Persistent rumors would have it that their dad had been in jail for everything from fraud to murder. How much of this was true, I didn't know.

Stephanie's mom was a nurse, and had remarried a couple of years ago. Stephanie liked her stepdad a lot. I had met Stephanie's mom a couple of times, but never her stepdad. All I knew about him was that he was a high school teacher.

I had no idea how Rob felt about his stepdad. Rob was a strange, withdrawn kind of kid who gave me the creeps. There were rumors that he had been involved with a bad crowd doing drugs in the city, and that the family came here to get him away from all that.

He hadn't made any friends since he started in my class, and didn't do anything to make friends either. He kept to himself, and Stephanie had told me that she hardly ever knew where he was or what he was doing.

"Too bad he's not interested in horses," said Rachel. "I assume he's not?"

I shook my head. "Not any more," I said. "Apparently they both used to ride when they were little. But now he sneers at his sister for bothering to work up a sweat cleaning stables in exchange for a few lousy rides."

We rode in silence for a while. The only thing breaking the silence was the lively chirping from the birds and the muted thumps of Quatana and Baggi's hooves. I inhaled the wonderful smell of pine needles and the warm summer day. Suddenly it dawned on me that I was experiencing the true meaning of "idyllic." I scratched Quatana's mane and smiled to myself in pure happiness. I didn't know, of course, that this was to be the last quiet day without any worries for a long time.

When we turned the corner into the farmyard after our ride, Stephanie was just getting off her bike outside the stable. She greeted Rachel in a somewhat shy way, but soon the ice was broken and they chatted like old friends.

90

"Eva has told me a lot about you," said Stephanie to Rachel, while we unsaddled the horses.

"Uh-oh, that doesn't sound too good. No horrible revelations, I hope?" Rachel pretended to be ruffled.

Stephanie shook her head. "Not at all. She told me about how the two of you and another girl exposed an arsonist last summer. That must have been really scary."

Rachel shuddered. "Scary is right," she said. "I don't ever want to experience that again. There is nothing more frightening than some lunatic who sneaks around in the night and sets fire to people's animal barns and stables. It was pure luck it ended as well as it did. This year I want a nice, quiet summer, without a criminal for miles around."

She disappeared into the stable to find the grooming tools.

When she came back out, I said, "Speaking of criminals, I believe there's enough of those around still, and not too far away either. Don't forget about all the burglaries and assaults that have been happening around here lately."

I grabbed a brush and started cleaning off dust from Quatana's legs. She snorted apprehensively and started stomping her forelegs. I patted her flank and said firmly, "Don't pretend you're ticklish, because I don't buy it. Stand still, do you hear?"

Quatana thrashed her head and neighed angrily, but at least she stood still while I continued brushing.

"Did you hear about that last burglary?" I said to Stephanie. "My mom called from the airport just to tell me about it."

"Yeah, I heard about it at the dentist," said Stephanie as she shuddered. "She and her assistant didn't talk about anything else, while I sat there like an idiot with my mouth wide open and only able to respond with strange noises when they asked me something. That poor old lady was knocked down, and all of her money and some jewelry were taken, they said. It's pretty bad when people can't even be safe in their own homes. I can't believe the police haven't found out who's doing this yet."

"But do they know for sure that the same person is behind all of

91

the burglaries?" Rachel turned away from Baggi, with the grooming brush up in the air. "I mean, it could be a coincidence..." She didn't get to finish, because Baggi did not at all like that she had quit brushing so abruptly. Before Rachel knew what was happening, the horse had reached for the brush with his muzzle and jerked it out of her hand. But he didn't seem to like the taste of it, because he dropped it quickly and stood there scowling, offended by it.

We couldn't help laughing at him. "Okay, okay, you slave driver," said Rachel, "I'll get on with the brushing. Just take it easy." She bent down to pick up the brush, and got a slobbery smack in the neck from Baggi, who seemed to think he should find out what she tasted like too.

"Yuck! That was one wet kiss," said Rachel as she wiped her neck off before she continued to groom Baggi again. "What was I saying before I was so brutally attacked?"

Stephanie, who had started washing the saddle, looked up from a tangle of straps and metal rings. "You were talking about coincidences," she said quietly.

"Oh yes," said Rachel. "I was just wondering how the police would know for sure that the same person is behind all the burglaries. As far as I know, they haven't found a single fingerprint."

"Apparently he leaves some kind of a sign," I said. "That's what my mom had heard, and the newspaper has mentioned something about it too."

"What kind of sign?" Rachel looked at me.

"I have no idea. Do you know, Stephanie?"

Stephanie shook her head without looking up. It was quiet for a moment, then Stephanie said with resignation: "I thought I knew this by now, which straps go where. But I've done it again! I've made the strangest, most crooked bridle in the world!" She held up the straps to show us. I went over to her and inspected the different parts.

"You've got parts from two different bridles," I said. "That's all that's wrong. If you loosen that strap there... I pointed. "And replace it with this one, then it'll be right."

A moment later the bridle looked like a bridle again. Rachel turned to Stephanie. "If I may give you a tip, she said, "it's easier if you take apart one bridle at a time and put it back together again before you do the next one. Then you won't risk getting them mixed up."

"That's a good idea," said Stephanie. "I'll remember that next time. Did any of you see what happened to the saddle soap?"

Rachel nodded. "You're sitting on it," she said. Stephanie got up quickly, and sure enough, there it was.

"And I was getting bothered by this rocky and uncomfortable seat," said Stephanie, and we all burst out laughing.

Before Stephanie went home for the night, we agreed to meet the next morning and get done with the stable work as early as we could, so we could go for a nice, long horseback ride together. It looked like we were going to have some good weather.

"If your brother would like to come too, he's more than welcome," said Rachel when Stephanie got on her bike to go home.

Stephanie just shook her head. "He doesn't want to do anything anymore," she said with a sad look. Then, before Rachel could say any more, she said goodbye and biked away.

Chapter 3

"Boy, I'm tired. I think I'll go to bed now," said Rachel with a big yawn.

"Me too. I can feel my eyelids sagging towards my knees," I said. "Besides, there's nothing good on TV tonight."

Rachel and I cooked lasagna and ate it while watching TV. That's a treat for me. My parents would never have let me do it. When it comes to that particular thing, they're hopelessly old-fashioned. They think dinner should be a family gathering. This is a time when we should be talking to each other rather than sitting around staring at the TV or reading the newspaper, according to them. Breakfast, on the other hand, is evidently not a family gathering. Then they both bury their heads in their own section of the paper and only mumble if I try to talk to them. But that's just fine with me, because I'm not really talkative in the morning either.

We turned off the TV, checked that the doors were locked, and walked quietly upstairs.

It felt as if I had only just fallen asleep when I was awakened by a strange noise. I sat up in bed all confused. I was so tired my head buzzed. Had I just dreamed that I heard something? No, there was the noise again. At first I thought the sound came from downstairs, and I felt a chill creeping up my back. But then I realized that the sound came from somewhere outside the house. Barking? Yes, it was a dog barking. But why did the noise sound so strange? I looked over toward my bedroom window, which was open a crack.

The window faced the farmyard and the stables. Suddenly the barking was mixed in with some other sound, and there was no mistaking that sound; the neighing of horses. Something was going on in the stable. Suddenly I was wide awake. Hurrying, I threw on whatever clothes were nearest, and stormed into Rachel's room. Her window faced out towards the back yard, so she hadn't heard anything.

"Rachel, wake up," I said and shook her.

She jumped up so fast that I almost fell over.

"Who... what..." she stammered, staring about wildly. Then she seemed to wake up, because she looked straight at me and said, "What's going on?"

"There's somebody in the stable," I said frantically. "There's a lot of neighing and barking out there. What if it's burglars?"

"Why would burglars bring a dog with them?" mumbled Rachel while she struggled to get her clothes on.

We tumbled down the stairs in a chaotic shuffle, stepped into the first shoes we found, and stormed out of the house and over to the stable. The stable door was closed and locked like it should be, but on the inside we were met with an ear-deafening noise. A loud mix of agitated neighing, stomping and wild barks from...

"Boris!" yelled Rachel when she got the door open. "What in the world are you doing in here?"

Boris jumped and danced around us, and barked so intensely his whole body was quivering. Then he seemed to suddenly realize that he was free, because he stopped barking and started running in a circle while his tail was wagging like a windshield wiper behind him.

By the time Rachel and I had calmed the horses down and checked that everything was fine in the stable, I felt fully awake. We closed and locked up the stable again, while Boris ran between our legs making gratifying little noises.

"He must have sneaked into the stable some time earlier in the evening and gone to sleep in one of the empty stalls without us noticing him," said Rachel, as she scratched the perpetrator behind the ears. He sure didn't look like some remorseful sinner, rather his eyes had an "oh-poor-little-me" expression.

"Poor Boris," I said.

"Woof!" said Boris and looked expectantly up at me.

"He's probably thirsty and hungry," Rachel reasoned. "We can't send him home without giving him something to eat first, otherwise he'll probably bark old Mr. Anderson right out of his bed when he gets home."

I agreed, and at that we both headed for the kitchen with Boris in tow. The door was wide open, so if any burglars had been around, they wouldn't even have had to break in. This place was pretty much saying "help yourself." The thought scared me, but I needn't have worried. There had not been any unwanted visitors while we were gone. The food money my parents had left for us was still in the kitchen cabinet where it belonged. The same was true for the ATM card. And the camera was sitting in the middle of the living room table, clearly visible to anyone who entered the room. Not very smart, perhaps... Of course nobody was going to break into our house, but just to be on the safe side, I decided to put the camera somewhere less visible. I put it under the table, so at least it couldn't be seen from the window.

Boris wolfed down some leftover meatloaf from the day before. Then he drained the bowl of water we had put out for him. A full and contented dog eventually headed home at an unhurried pace. The last thing I saw of him before he disappeared was the bushy tail wagging like a banner behind him.

Rachel and I locked the door and went upstairs to go back to bed.

"If there are any more dogs lying about in the stable, they will just have to stay there until morning," said Rachel as she yawned. "I am not getting up again, no matter how much racket they make."

"Isn't that typical of Boris, though?" I said. "That dog is always getting into trouble. He deserves to be shooed home with a kick in the butt, but instead that rascal looks at us with his beseeching eyes and voilá, the next thing you know he's getting treats fit for a king."

"The next time I'll pour a bucket of water over him instead," promised Rachel.

"Ha!" I said. "Sure you will. You're a bigger sucker for Boris than I am!"

"I guess you're right," said Rachel. "Good night and sweet dreams — about barking dogs and other fun things."

I didn't fall asleep for a long time. At first I was thinking about Stephanie having to move here because her mom and stepdad wanted Rob out of the city. That couldn't have been easy for her. Had anyone asked her how she felt about moving, I wondered? I knew she missed her old friends, and it must feel like it was all for nothing, having moved to give her brother a better life, when he was so crabby and testy and impossible to talk to. Maybe being an only child was not so bad after all? I had always wanted siblings, but after an accident, my mom wasn't able to have any more children, so there was no use thinking about it. Regardless, I would not have wanted a brother like Rob, that's for sure.

Then my thoughts went to the burglaries and assaults that had been happening in town over the last few weeks. Rachel and I had watched the local news on TV earlier in the evening and gotten more information about the last burglary. What Stephanie had heard at the dentist was right. The poor old lady had been brutally struck down in her own home, and they had taken her money and jewelry. It didn't sound like the police had very many leads in the case, but they hinted at this "sign" that the burglar had left. According to the news reporter, identical signs had been found at the site of the other recent burglaries, and therefore they were pretty certain that the same person or persons were behind all of them. How someone could be so completely without conscience that they would attack a defenseless elderly person was more than I could comprehend.

When I finally fell asleep, I had a fantastic dream, fortunately with no dogs or attackers. I was out riding Aron. We were in a kind of fairy tale landscape with incredibly beautiful trees and flowers made of glass, or maybe it was candy, I couldn't tell. Aron floated forward in rhythmic, wavy movements, and it was just wonderful

97

to sit on his back. In the dream he could even talk, and he told me how much fun it was to be my horse, though he teasingly added that I could be pretty dumb sometimes. But after all I was only a human, and based on that I was apparently as good as any horse could expect. We agreed that we were pretty lucky, both of us, to have each other. It was a wonderful dream, and I was really sad to wake up to the intrusive ringing of my alarm clock.

But then I remembered the ride that Rachel, Stephanie and I were going to take, so I pushed myself out of bed and stumbled toward the bathroom. Of course right at that moment Rachel came into the hall too. I squinted sleepily at her and she started laughing.

"I think I'll go and get the camera," she said. "We could make a video called "The world's smallest eyes." I stuck my tongue out at her and hurried into the bathroom before she could do anything about her threat.

Chapter 4

"Hey, Stephanie! You look like you sold your horse and didn't get paid." Stephanie started at my voice. She was standing in front of the stable door, and was obviously so preoccupied by her own thoughts that she hadn't heard us coming. She seemed tired and out of sorts. Maybe a dog woke her up too? Then she forced a smile and said hi. Rachel looked searchingly at her and asked if something was the matter.

"No, never mind, it's nothing really. Just a lot of arguing and noise at home last night. That's the way it is almost every day nowadays, so it's nice to get out of there."

"Is it Rob?" I asked with hesitation.

Stephanie nodded. "He's totally impossible, cranky and difficult, and when my mom asks where he's been all night, he refuses to answer. My stepdad, Steve, grounded him last night, but then he just climbed out the window and disappeared. I don't understand what's wrong with him. I've tried to talk to him, but he just walks away."

Stephanie had tears in her eyes. I felt so sorry for her. Fortunately her spirits lifted while we were taking care of the horses, and we rode off in good spirits, I on Quatana, Rachel on Baggi, and Stephanie on Primanka, one of the calmest horses in the stable.

Our good mood didn't last long, unfortunately. Usually there isn't much traffic on the road where we were riding, so we were walking along at an easy pace, side by side by side, when we suddenly heard the roar from a powerful car engine a little way behind us.

"There's a car coming," yelled Rachel, "over on the right,

everybody!" We barely made it before the car came shooting toward us. I turned around in the saddle and was struck with fear.
The car came at us fast, and didn't show any sign of slowing
down, rather the opposite. It shot past us with minimal clearance.
Two people were in the car, and I just got a glimpse of the passenger, a seventeen-year-old boy whom I knew. He belonged to a
rather questionable gang, which used to hang around downtown
and start trouble. The driver was probably another one from the
same gang, I guessed.

"What a couple of idiots," Rachel screamed in outrage when the
car disappeared behind a turn in the road, and we were able to hear
ourselves again. "They passed so close to us it was pure luck that
none of the horses swerved. Shoot, I wish I had seen the license
number. Did any of you get it?"

Stephanie and I both said no. It had all happened so fast.

"But I think I know the passenger," I said. "That is, I can't remember his name, but I know which gang he belongs to. They're
always dressed in black and call themselves The Panthers."

"People like that shouldn't be allowed to drive," Rachel said angrily. "Maybe we ought to... Oh-my-God, they're coming back!"

We heard the roar of an engine, and then the car showed up
again, heading straight for us.

"They're going to run us over!" screamed Stephanie.

"Get off the road! Head for the trees, where they can't follow,"
commanded Rachel.

Stephanie and I didn't need to be asked twice. We turned the
horses and directed them toward the trees and bushes that grew
way back off the shoulder of the road. We just made it before the
car swept past on the road behind us, so close I could feel the air
suction. With triumphant honking, which made the horses jump,
the car disappeared back toward town. I turned around in the saddle and managed to just barely get a glimpse of it before it was
gone in a cloud of dust.

Stephanie refused to get back on the road. She was scared to death
that the car would come back again. So was I, to be perfectly hon-

est. The two people in the car had given the impression that they were totally wild. Maybe they were high on drugs? If so, there was no telling what they might be capable of.

"They probably wouldn't have run us down," tried Rachel in an attempt to calm us down. "They were just trying to scare us..."

"Well, they managed that!" said Stephanie in a quiver. "Look at me, my legs are trembling so hard I can't keep them still, and I feel sick!"

We spent at least ten minutes trying to calm down not only each other but the horses, while we listened for any sound indicating that the car was coming back. But it was all quiet now.

Finally we dared get back on the road, because it was impossible to ride on the shoulder of the road on this stretch. The ground was too rugged and rocky, with lots of holes and ditches that the horses could easily step into and get hurt.

We didn't relax until we made it safely to a riding trail five minutes later. I regretted not taking the cell phone with me, so we could call the police and report the speeding drivers right away. There didn't seem to be much point in doing it now, because what could we prove? We hadn't managed to get the license number of the car, and all of us had different theories about what kind of car it was. The only thing we agreed on was that the car was white and probably not new. In the end we decided we might as well forget the whole thing and enjoy our ride, and that became easier the further into the woods we got. After a while the episode seemed kind of unreal, more like a bad dream than something that actually had happened. Even so, I wasn't completely able to shake off a creepy feeling that this was only the beginning, and that there was more trouble in store for us.

Chapter 5

The unusual quiet was the first thing that told me something was wrong. Normally when I brought Mr. Anderson the library books I checked out for him he would stand in the kitchen window waiting for me. And Boris would come running across the yard to greet me in his usual, overly delighted way.

Today, however, the house seemed totally deserted. I thought it strange. It was a regular understanding that I would pick up books for Mr. Anderson once a week, which is why I had biked to the library as soon as Rachel, Stephanie and I got back from our ride.

I parked the bike and walked uncertainly toward the front door. I knocked on the door, but there was no response. Wasn't Mr. Anderson home? I tried the doorknob. The door was unlocked, and slid open with a slight squeak. I poked my head in the doorway and called, "Hello, Mr. Anderson; it's me, Eva!"

There was no answer, but I heard Boris barking. It sounded like the barking came from the basement. I thought of Mr. Anderson and his poor legs. Had he actually dared to go down in the basement? What if he had fallen and hurt himself? I quickly went into the entrance, and was heading for the basement door when I happened to glance over toward the living room door. It was open, and I could see someone lying on the floor in there, quite still. It was Mr. Anderson; he must have had an attack of some sort.

I hurried into the living room. The sight that met me made me drop the bag of books, spilling them out onto the floor. I had to restrain myself from screaming out loud when I saw the blood trickling from the old man's head. He must have stumbled and fallen, hitting his head against something. Maybe a table? He was lying on his side without moving at all. Was he dead? My vision blurred and black spots floated in front of me. I felt warm and funny in the head.

Man, I'd better not faint, I thought, and sat down abruptly on the floor next to Mr. Anderson. While waves of nausea almost overtook me, I reached my hand out and placed my fingertips on Mr. Anderson's neck to feel for a pulse. If I hadn't felt one, I don't know what I would have done. But luckily, I soon felt the rapid, irregular pulse against my fingers and realized that Mr. Anderson was alive.

I knew I had to get help fast. I struggled to my feet, which didn't feel like mine at all. They were shaking uncontrollably and felt as if they had a will of their own. But they carried me, and that's all that mattered at the moment.

I looked around for the phone, and that's when I realized that something else was totally wrong here. There was chaos everywhere around me, couch pillows scattered on the floor, the contents of drawers and cabinets in disarray all over the place. And on one of the walls was sprayed a strange symbol. It looked like a snake curling up on itself. Well, actually it reminded me of the kind of doodles that graffiti artists spray on walls and buses. I suddenly remembered that the burglars, who had been operating in the area, had been said to leave a symbol in every house they had burglarized.

Burglary! The burglars have been here, and they must have struck down Mr. Anderson, I thought, shocked. I must call the police... and get an ambulance, fast! Okay, calm down, I said to myself. I looked around and spotted the phone on the end table. I picked up the receiver and started dialing the emergency number before I realized that I didn't have a dial tone. Darn! I slammed the receiver back on, lifted it back up and waited. Nothing. Why wasn't the phone working? I looked at it, and then followed the cord with my eyes, toward the jack in the wall. Then I knew I could just forget about calling from this phone. The phone cord had been cut, and was curled up on the floor like a dead worm.

A feeling of panic washed over me. What was I going to do? I had to get help for Mr. Anderson, but I couldn't just leave him.

What if he got worse while I was gone? What if his heart stopped, and no one was there to do CPR? Oh, I wish he didn't live so far away from everybody!

Our farm was actually the nearest neighbor to Mr. Anderson. Rachel and Stephanie were in the stable by now. If I could just get a message to them… but how?

I felt like sitting down and crying out loud, like Boris was doing in the basement. That's it, Boris! I had forgotten all about him. His desperate barking had been like a dim background noise to my own panic, but the sound had not registered with me. The shock of finding Mr. Anderson on the floor, bloody and unconscious, had pushed aside everything else.

I got an idea that I hoped would work. There was a pen and some paper by the phone. Quickly I scribbled down a message for Rachel about what had happened. I checked Mr. Anderson's pulse again. It was still rapid and somewhat irregular. Wasn't an irregular pulse a dangerous sign? I almost panicked again, but managed to pull myself together.

Quickly I ran to the basement door and let Boris out. He was overjoyed to get out. He was quite uncontrollable, though, and I regretted having let him loose. But after he ran into the living room to greet his master, he seemed to understand that something was wrong. Surely his owner wasn't supposed to lie like that, completely still on the floor? Boris carefully sniffed him. Maybe it was the blood, but Boris suddenly started whimpering with his tail between his legs.

I dragged Boris out into the entrance. With numb, shaking hands, I fastened the note to his collar. Then I pulled him outside. Boris looked uncertainly at me, but his tail started moving slightly again.

"Boris," I said pleadingly. "Go to my dad. Go to Dad and get hamburgers! Yum, yum, hamburgers!"

Boris looked at me. He tilted his head and lifted his ears slightly, but made no move to run toward our farm. I felt helpless. This would never work.

"Hamburgers!" I said again, as excitedly as I could. "Yum, yum. Boris, go get hamburgers! Lots of hamburgers!"

"Woof!" said Boris excitedly, and then he shot like a bullet across the fields in the direction of our farm.

I let out a deep sigh of relief and hurried back inside to Mr. Anderson. Should I bandage the wound? Anderson had a first-aid kit in the kitchen. I got a sterile compress and put it gently over the wound. Then I grabbed a pillow and carefully lifted Mr. Anderson's head onto it. I seemed to remember that it was important to keep the patient warm, especially if there was a possibility of shock, so I also spread a blanket over him.

What else could I do? I had taken a first-aid class the year before, but now that it was for real I felt like my brain was all mush and I couldn't remember much of anything. Talk to the patient? I didn't know if there was any point in talking to an unconscious person, but it seemed better than just sitting there worrying. I had already started thinking of all the things that could stop Boris from reaching the farm with the note I had written. Normally he would start barking like crazy outside the kitchen window, and if he did, Rachel and Stephanie would hear him. But what if they didn't? What if he lost the note on his way there, what if he saw a cat and started chasing after it instead, what if...

Stop it, I told myself, - this is no good. I took Mr. Anderson's hand resolutely. It was limp and didn't move at all, and there was no response when I gently squeezed it. I felt very awkward, but continued to hold his hand while I talked about everything and nothing. My mind was a complete chaos, and I'm sure there was no rhyme or reason to anything I said. I just let the words pour out of me so I wouldn't have to think.

Suddenly I jumped. Had Mr. Anderson moved? I looked at his hand, which was as limp as a rag doll in my hand. Then my heart skipped a beat. Mr. Anderson's fingers squeezed my hand for a second, and he gave out a barely audible moan. Then his hand went limp again.

"Mr. Anderson," I said quietly. "Can you hear me? It's Eva. You were attacked, but you'll be fine. Help is on the way."

I hoped it was true. Before I could say anything more, Mr. Anderson moved slightly again. His eyes opened and he looked

into the room, but it didn't seem like he saw me or registered anything around him. The whole thing lasted only a few seconds,
And then his eyes slid shut again, while he mumbled something in
a barely audible voice. "Bert... it was Bert..." I thought he said,
but I wasn't sure. I tried to talk to him, but there was no response.
He was unconscious again, and now I thought his breathing was
getting irregular as well. It was with enormous relief I registered
the piercing sound of sirens from an approaching ambulance.

The paramedics worked quickly and efficiently. Mr. Anderson
was on his way to the hospital in less than five minutes after they
arrived. A police car had followed closely behind them, and I had
to give a short explanation of what had happened. Then they started their crime scene investigation while I was sent home. They
told me they might want to talk to me more later, but I hardly registered them saying it. I was completely numb as I rode my bike
home, and just felt like crying. All I could think of was getting
home and into the stable, where I could bury my head in a wonderful, soft horse mane and forget everything that had happened.
But I knew that I could never forget it.

Chapter 6

"Are you saying you didn't remember to tell the police what Mr. Anderson said?" Rachel looked at me in disbelief. She and I were sitting in Quatana's stall, talking. Stephanie had just gone home on her bike.

I nodded sheepishly. Next to me Quatana was eating a mouthful of pellets and crunching so loudly it echoed in the stall. I reached my hand up and stroked her across her forehead. She snorted and shook her head. I had to smile. She was so cute standing there.

Her mane was dry again now. A little while ago it had been completely wet from my tears. Rachel and Stephanie must have thought I was out of my mind when I came storming into the stable after leaving my bike flat out in the farmyard. They started interrogating me about what had happened to Mr. Anderson, but I just shook my head and ran into Quatana's stall. In there I did exactly what I had felt like doing during the entire bike ride home. I cried into her mane, sobbing and letting my tears run freely, until I felt completely empty. Quatana had stood quite still and kindly accepted my outburst without a grumble. Sometimes both she and Aron love to nip at my hair or lightly pinch when they feel like it, but she made no attempts at any of that while I was crying. It was almost like she understood that I wasn't up to fooling around right then.

Later, when I had calmed down, I told them everything that had happened, and how horrible it was to sit there totally helpless, without knowing if the ambulance was on the way or not.

"It was a streak of genius to come up with the idea of the hamburgers," Rachel said admiringly, and gave Quatana a light smack on the behind, to get her to move over a little. The horse had come very close to stepping on her hand. "You should have heard the noise Boris made outside when he came. We were wondering if the poor dog had completely lost it. When we came out of the stable, he ran back and forth underneath the kitchen window barking like a maniac. At first Stephanie and I thought maybe somebody had tried to break in, and that Boris had seen him, but then I saw the note fastened to his collar. Since the note mentioned both 'assault' and 'seriously injured,' I called for both ambulance and police."

I nodded. "I told the police what had happened, and then they sent me home. But my mind was so cloudy, I totally forgot to tell them that Mr. Anderson had tried to say something."

Rachel, Stephanie and I had twisted and turned the words at least a thousand times before Stephanie went home, but we couldn't figure it out. Was "Bert" a name? We didn't know anyone called that. Was it part of a name? First name or last name? We tried several possibilities; Albert, Bertram, and several other names that we thought up and some which definitely do not exist, like Shortbert and Smallbert.

"It may not even be a name," Stephanie finally said. "Mr. Anderson may have meant something entirely different. If he was at all aware of what he was saying."

"You're right, it could have meant anything," I said, discouraged. "He may even have just tried to say the man was a brute, as far as we know."

After that, Stephanie said she wanted to go home. She didn't feel well; her tummy was hurting. And she really didn't look so well either. Maybe the shock from earlier in the day was still affecting her.

"What a day!" I said to Rachel when we had locked up the stable for the night and were walking toward the house. First we were almost run over by some crazy drivers, and then I ran into a real burglary and assault right afterwards.

"Mr. Anderson was sure lucky to have you come by just then,"

108

said Rachel. "Who knows how long he might have lain there with-out help if you hadn't?"

I shuddered at the thought. Then I thought of something. "Boris!" I said. "Where is he?"

"Darn!" said Rachel, "I totally forgot about him! He was right behind me when I ran inside to call the ambulance, but I haven't seen him since."

"He probably ran back home," I said. "Maybe we should go over there and get him. He won't understand when Mr. Anderson doesn't let him in. We can't let poor Boris go hungry while his owner is in the hospital."

"I'll go and get Boris, and in the meantime you can call the hos-pital and ask how Mr. Anderson is doing," suggested Rachel.

But when we got inside, we saw that Rachel didn't have to go over to Mr. Anderson's house. On the living room couch we found a black and white dog, all stretched out and sleeping peacefully. He woke up when we walked in, and his tail started wagging ex-pectantly. It knocked down a plant, making the pot break into pieces on the floor.

"Oh, Boris!" I said, slightly bummed out, but I couldn't help laughing.

"Woof!" said Boris with anticipation.

"He's probably hungry," said Rachel. "Take him to the kitchen and give him something to eat. He's still waiting for those ham-burgers you promised him!"

"Woof!" said Boris again, and followed me more than willingly into the kitchen. It's about time they give me some service around here, he seemed to be saying. I agreed. He had certainly earned some hamburgers. But unfortunately I didn't have any. Boris would have to do with hot dogs instead.

Chapter 7

Sleep didn't come easily that night. First of all I had a guilty conscience. Mom had called. She and Dad were having a great time. She just wanted to check how Rachel and I were doing, and I had lied shamelessly, saying everything was fine and nothing had happened worth worrying about. I tried to tell myself that it was a necessary white lie so my mom wouldn't get all upset. If I had told the truth, she might just have ended her vacation right then and there and taken the first plane home. But it was really hard to keep it up when she asked if I had remembered the library books for Mr. Anderson. Actually, I didn't need to lie about that, because I had. I just didn't mention that he wouldn't be reading them for some time.

Mr. Anderson was the main reason I couldn't sleep. I had called the hospital, hoping he was okay and awake and able to tell them who had attacked him. But the hospital didn't have any good news for me. At first they wouldn't say anything, because I was not a relative, but after a lot of pleading and explanations that it was I who had found him, that we were next-door neighbors, that I was looking after his dog and so on, they finally gave me some answers. When I hung up, I kind of wished they hadn't. Mr. Anderson's condition was critical but stable, whatever that meant. When I asked in a frightened voice if that meant that Mr. Anderson would die, the voice at the other end had just said in a friendly tone, "The doctors are doing all they can for him. We will just have to wait, and hope for the best."

While I was lying there tossing and turning, I thought about Boris, who was sleeping in the kitchen, in blissful ignorance that his owner might never come home. I couldn't bear to think about it. Then I felt anger well up inside me. What kind of people would, without scruples or shame, break into the home of an elderly, defenseless person and strike him down, not caring whether he lived or died? If Mr. Anderson's condition was critical now that he was being taken care of by the hospital staff, then surely he would have died if I hadn't stopped by and found him in time. At least I hoped I had been in time.

I must have fallen asleep at some point, because I know I dreamed a lot of scary and unpleasant things that I didn't remember the details of when I woke up the next morning. My head was as heavy as lead as I reluctantly stumbled out of bed to start a new day.

Boris was a contented participant in the stable that morning. He seemed a little confused that we suddenly accepted having him with us night and day, as we usually chased him back home as soon as he came over for some fun. But there was no doubt that he enjoyed being with us.

The horses scowled skeptically at him when he came into the stable, and Chareb, the most valuable stallion we have, snapped at his tail, which he had carelessly let slip through the bars of the horse's stall. But other than that, things went fine. Quatana greeted me with contented neighing, and I went into her stall to cuddle with her before I started my work in the stable. "Hello, girl," I said quietly, scratching her forehead. "Do you want to go riding again today?" Quatana blew her warm breath down my arm. I took that as a yes. I was almost done grooming her when Stephanie showed up. She looked like she hadn't slept for several weeks. Was she still feeling sick?

"No, no," said Stephanie when I asked her. "I've just been up most of the night, because Rob disappeared last night. My mom and Steve go back and forth between worry and rage, and the whole atmosphere is just unbearable."

"Do you mean he's run away?"

Stephanie nodded. "He told me he was going to stay at a friend's house for a couple of days, then he packed a bag and split.

111

And now my mom is mad at me because I didn't stop him, or at least ask him what his friend's name is and where he lives. Now we don't have a clue where Rob is. I'm just glad I got out of the house before they got up this morning, or they might not have let me to come to the stable."

"It's not fair to blame you for Rob running away," said Rachel. "How were you supposed to stop him, by knocking him down, maybe?"

"Right now that's exactly what I feel like doing," said Stephanie bitterly. "But let's talk about something else. Which of the stalls should I clean first?"

We worked in silence for a while. Then Stephanie said, "I must be completely out of it today. I totally forgot to ask if you know how Mr. Anderson is doing."

"I called the hospital this morning again," I said, "They told me that his condition is serious but stable. I think that's a little better than critical, which is what they said last night."

"So then he's getting better," said Stephanie happily.

"Let's hope he wakes up soon and tells them who attacked him," said Rachel.

Stephanie didn't say anything. She looked glum again, and I figured she was thinking about Rob and the problems back home.

"This has been a great ride," said Stephanie excitedly. "I'm getting more and more fond of riding all the time, and it's so much fun to have someone to go with."

It was two days later. Rob had not come home yet, but we had at least gotten one bit of good news. Mr. Anderson was out of danger. He was still unconscious, but the doctors thought that he would wake up within a few days.

The police had stopped by to talk to me again. They wanted to know if I remembered anything else that I hadn't told them. But I hadn't thought of anything. They already knew that Mr. Anderson had said "Bert" or something like that, because I had called and told them the same night I had forgotten, after I got home.

"Bert"... There was something about that word, it reminded me of something, but I couldn't think of what it was. I had a feeling that I should know what Mr. Anderson had meant, but every time I tried to think really hard of what it was, it slipped away. It really bugged me.

We were on our way home after a long ride to the beach. All three of us had been rather tired and grouchy in the morning when we headed out from the farmyard, but there's no better cure for that than taking off at a gallop along a soft beach. We found a cove with no people where we could let the horses gallop.

"Boris would have liked this place," Rachel commented as we raced each other along the edge of the water.

We hadn't wanted to risk taking Boris with us on such a long ride. You never knew what he might get into. On the way to the beach we had to pass through several residential areas, and the mere thought of having a mischievous and imaginative dog running around the horses in traffic and everything, was enough to make us leave Boris at home. We put him in an empty stall in the stable, with plenty of water and food, so he was not deprived, though he himself seemed to think he was. He whimpered pitifully when we shut the door to leave.

We'll have to make it up to him when we get back, I thought to myself.

"Trouble ahead!"

We were riding down a small gravel road in a residential area when we spotted three teenagers coming in from a side road in front of us. They started walking down the road with their backs toward us. I recognized one of them as the passenger in the car that had almost run us down a couple of days ago. One of the others was possibly the driver, I wasn't sure, but since there's a total of five members in the Panthers the driver could just as well have been one of the two who wasn't in front of us now.

We held the horses back while I made Rachel and Stephanie aware of who was in front of us. Stephanie went as pale as a sheet and looked like she just wanted to disappear into a hole in the ground, if there had been one big enough for her and Primanka. I didn't feel all that brave myself, either, but Rachel said, "Relax; they can't do anything to us. If they try something we can easily ride away from them."

She was right, of course. Even so, I was sitting on Quatana's back and just hoping that they wouldn't turn around and see us. And they may not have, if Baggi hadn't suddenly lost his patience. I guess he was wondering why in the world we were just sitting there not moving at all for no good reason. This was plain boring! And he let us know as much with a neigh that vibrated between the houses.

The three in front of us turned around instantly and saw us. Oh no, I thought, they're going to come toward us!

But fortunately they just gave us the finger and some ugly threatening faces and left it at that. Then they rounded a corner and vanished. I was very relieved that they were gone.

Quatana and Baggi stood tethered outside the stable, while I was busy throwing a ball for Boris. Rachel was in the kitchen preparing a casserole we were going to eat later. Stephanie had gone home to find out if there was any news of Rob. The way he'd been behaving lately, maybe the family should just be happy he was staying away, I thought, and threw a ball into the stable wall so that it bounced back. Boris jumped on it with great delight. He was full of energy after having been locked up all day. He came running toward me with his tail wagging, hoping I would throw the ball again.

Quatana watched us with a guarded look, while Baggi stood dozing peacefully after his outing. Quatana almost looked like she might want to join our ball play. I threw the ball into the stable wall again, but this time I miscalculated badly. Instead of bouncing back into the farmyard, the ball went into a curve, hit the ground and rolled right underneath Baggi. Boris darted gleefully after the ball. Baggi, however, was quite unprepared for a rambunctious dog interrupting his afternoon nap, and jumped irritably. He aimed a kick with his foreleg at Boris, and just barely missed.

114

"Boris, come here!" I shouted frantically, and Boris came running with the ball in his mouth, happily ignorant of having been within an inch of Baggi's powerful kick.

Baggi snorted angrily after him and stomped his legs to demonstrate his displeasure. Then he quieted down and went back to snoozing.

Boris and I continued our play for a little while longer. Rachel came running out of the house, all in a fluster, and interrupted us.

"Eva, there's been another burglary, just this afternoon," she shouted. "They just said so on the news. The police found the same symbol this time too."

I felt a chill. "Who... how..." I stammered. "Was anyone hurt? Did they say where?"

"They mentioned a street name. What was it... oh yeah, Linden Street, I think it was. The elderly lady who lives in the house was just out for an errand, and when she got back the house had been turned upside down. The thieves took money and various valuables."

"Good thing the lady was out," I said, while my mind was churning. "Linden Street, you said? We just rode by that street this afternoon."

"That gang we saw, Rachel said fervently. "The Panthers. Do you think they might have something to do with the burglary?"

I thought about it. "It wouldn't surprise me," I said slowly. "I know several of them have been involved in criminal acts before. But the fact that we saw them there doesn't prove anything."

While we took Quatana and Baggi into the stable, we discussed the issue further, but didn't get any closer to a solution. We couldn't very well call the police on such miniscule grounds that we had seen three members of the Panthers gang in the area. Rachel suddenly remembered that she wanted to buy fruit before the supermarket closed, so she borrowed my bike and took off to the store.

While she was gone, I filled the boxes with hay for Quatana, Baggi and the other horses who didn't go in the pasture. Then I sat down in a corner of Quatana's stall and watched as she chowed down the juicy, yellowish straws of hay.

I must have fallen asleep, because before I knew it, Rachel was standing in the doorway calling my name. I scampered to my feet, all dizzy and sleepy. Her face was all red with excitement.

"Has something happened?" I asked, disoriented.

"I should say so," said Rachel. "I had no idea buying apples and bananas could be so useful."

I stared at her completely perplexed, and she started laughing.

"Guess who I saw at the market?" she asked, without waiting for any suggestions from me. "The three guys we saw near Linden Street," she said. "And two others."

"Well, then you saw the entire Panthers gang," I said and yawned, "but what about it? Did they attack the cashier lady or break into the ATM machine?"

Rachel shook her head. "No, nothing like that," she said. "They were just standing there, hanging out. But then one of them moved to go and buy something at the newspaper stand; the guy who was the passenger in the car that harassed us. And one of the others called after him, 'Buy me a Coke, Berry.' I didn't react to that, but when Berry didn't answer, he called again, in a more sarcastic tone, 'Pretty please, Bertil dearest,' and at that Berry got furious and said that if he used that idiotic name one more time he could just forget about the Coke, not to mention his teeth."

I stared at Rachel, completely dumbfounded. Berry... Bertil... Bert... "Of course!" I screamed. "Bertil... that's what Mr. Anderson was trying to say!"

"That's what I think, too," said Rachel.

"Well, what are we waiting for?" I shouted. "C'mon, let's call the police right away. Then the case of the burglaries will probably be solved in no time!"

We raced each other to the house with an excited Boris hot on our heels. He thought this was another fun game, and looked rather disappointed when all we wanted was the stupid telephone. He sighed deeply and lay down on the floor, while Rachel dialed the number of the police station.

116

Chapter 9

The next morning, when we turned on the radio, we were happy to hear the news that five young people had been taken into custody, on suspicion of being behind the burglaries and assaults.

Rachel's face was one big smile. "Am I a clever detective or what?"

I threw a kitchen towel at her. "It's called luck, I said teasingly. "Nothing more.

"Lucky is as lucky does," recited Rachel and brushed Boris aside as he tried to sneak up on the kitchen table to look for missed treats. "Oh no, you rascal, that's enough food for you. We can't have you looking like a balloon when your owner comes home. Now we're going to the stable, and you are not going to upset the horses, you hear?"

Boris tilted his head and looked at her with that innocent look of his. He might as well have said, "Me, upset the horses? I would never do that!"

When we went into the stable, Stephanie was already there. She looked a little better than the day before.

I asked if Rob had come home again. She nodded.

"Yes, he came home late last night. I think he had expected a real bawl-out, but Mom and Steve were so relieved to have him home safe that they just hugged him and sent him off to bed. I'm sure there'll be a row later, though, when he wakes up, so I made sure to get out of there early. Then they can scream at each other all they want without me having to listen to it."

"Did you hear...?" I started, but was interrupted by fierce neighing. I turned around. Quatana was standing in her stall looking reproachfully at me. What kind of nonsense was this? Were

117

we just going to stand there blabbering all day, showing no concern for a poor horse who was hungry and needed company?

I laughed and went into her stall. "You're sure impatient today," I said and ruffled her mane. She snorted and threw her head, making me back up so I wouldn't get hit.

"Hey, quit it!" I said firmly. "That's no way to say good morning! Here, have an apple. Will you be nice now?"

Quatana nodded contentedly and gobbled up the apple I had given her.

"Make note of that apple there," said Rachel humorously to Stephanie. "It's a part of the detective work that solved a crime wave."

Stephanie stared at her incomprehensibly, and Rachel had to explain what had happened at the market, and how it had led to the Panthers being arrested.

"That's fantastic!" Stephanie looked as if she had won the lottery and the sweepstakes all in one day. "You have no idea how worried I was that..."

She stopped. "No, it was nothing," she said quickly. "Anyway, that's great news. But we'd better start cleaning the stalls, or we won't be able to go riding today."

We did get in a ride, though it wasn't a very long one. We kept to the fields around the farm, and just made a short trip over to Mr. Anderson's house to make sure everything was in order. Boris came with us too. That was not intentional. Rachel had tried to shut him in the stable, but that little dickens saw it coming, and managed to escape every attempt at capture. Finally we tried to corner him, but it just ended with us, all sweaty and tired, reluctantly accepting that he had us outmaneuvered. Lucky for the police that Boris was not a burglar. They would never have been able to catch him!

Spirits were high that night when Rachel and I went to bed. Another call to the hospital had confirmed that Mr. Anderson really was getting better. He had been awake for a short moment, and had asked for Boris. According to the nurse Rachel had talked to,

118

chances were pretty good that he would recover without any permanent injury.

My mom had called, too, and this time I could tell her everything was fine without lying too much. She and Dad were still having the time of their lives, and I had to listen to a long monologue about Rome and Spanish stairs and I don't know what, before her calling card ran out of minutes and she said a hasty goodbye.

That night I was really tired, and went to sleep quickly. Even my dream was sweet. Aron was a little foal again, and he and I were racing each other across a soft clover meadow. In my dream I could run just as fast as the long legged foal, and it was a fantastic feeling to speed through the summer landscape, side by side with the most gorgeous little horse in the world.

A loud bang and shattering glass brutally pulled me out of my dreamland. I sat up in bed, disoriented. What's happening? Boris was in the kitchen, barking like a maniac. I jumped out of bed and walked unsteadily toward the door. What in the world was that dog up to now?

Out in the hall I almost collided with Rachel. "Did you hear that bang?" she said "What do you think it was?"

"I guess Boris must have knocked something over," I said. "Let's go down and find out. It sounds like he's lost his mind down there!"

When we came into the kitchen, we quickly saw that we had mistrusted Boris for no reason. I stopped dead in the door and just stared. I couldn't believe my own eyes. The kitchen window was broken and there was shattered glass all over the floor. In the middle of the biggest mess of glass was a big piece of brick. It had landed frighteningly close to the blanket where Boris had been lying.

Boris stopped barking when we showed up at the kitchen door.

"Stay!" Rachel said firmly to him. We were scared to death he would get his paws all cut up by the sharp glass pieces.

To our great surprise, Boris actually obeyed. Rachel quickly got some shoes on, stepped in between the glass pieces, and lifted Boris out of the danger zone. We checked his paws, and happily determined that he was not hurt.

"Who on earth would throw a stone through our window? And why?" said Rachel after we had crawled into two chairs in the living room a little later. Boris had gone back to sleep on the couch. We didn't have the heart to chase him back down on the floor.

I shook my head. We had discussed the issue back and forth already.

"I wish the police would get here soon," I said. "This is just too scary. What if the people who did it come back?"

"I doubt it," stated Rachel. "If the plan was to break into the house, Boris's barking would have scared them away."

We hadn't touched anything in the kitchen, because the police officer Rachel had talked to on the phone had instructed us to leave everything as it was until they got someone out to investigate.

It was morning before anyone came. Rachel and I were still sitting in our chairs. We didn't feel there was much point in going to bed, because we knew we wouldn't be able to sleep anyway.

I guess I must have dozed off for a while, because when the doorbell suddenly rang, I really jumped. Outside was a friendly female police officer. She took some pictures, both in the kitchen and outside the house. Whatever else she did in the kitchen, I have no idea, because to Rachel's and my disappointment she asked us to wait in the living room while she completed her investigation.

She had the brick in a bag when she came back to us. In a different bag was a folded paper. "I'll take these with me," she said. "We will of course do our best, but unfortunately it's not very likely that we'll find out who the perpetrator is. Most likely it was a group of teenagers who were bored and wanted some excitement. It's bad, of course, but unfortunately these things happen now and then."

"Why do you think it is just a prank?" demanded Rachel.

"Because of the note. Typical kids, trying to be dramatic. We've seen similar things lots of times."

"Note?" We looked at her without comprehension.

"Yes, there was a note taped underneath the brick. It says: "We know it was you! This is just the beginning!"

Chapter 10

"Not in a million years do I believe that brick was just a random prank!" said Rachel, while we were grooming the horses a couple of hours later. Stephanie hadn't shown up yet.

"Me neither," I said. "I have a feeling the threat was for real, even if the police don't take it seriously."

The police officer had reassured us that it was not very likely that the vandals would come back. She assumed they had gotten scared by their own actions, and would be staying far away, especially now that they knew there was a dog in the house.

Before she left, she had helped us contact a glassworker who would come and fix the window. He came within half an hour, and when he left again the kitchen was back to normal. He had even been nice enough to sweep up and remove all the shattered glass pieces.

"'We know it was you!' So what? What was us?" pondered Rachel aloud while she let the grooming brush slide across Chareb's back in a long, slow motion. Chareb was not in a very good mood today, so Rachel had problems getting him to stand still. Suddenly he stretched his head back and snapped at her arm.

"Stop it, you bully!" Rachel smacked him on the neck. "I think you must have been indoors too long. What you need is to blow off some steam."

"My dad said we can't ride him," I warned her. "He has too many stallion whims. The only rider he shows any respect for is my mom."

"Too bad," sighed Rachel. "He's a fantastic horse. It must be a dream to fly forward on his back."

"More likely you would fly straight into a ditch," I said, laughing. "He's pretty quick about ridding himself of unwanted baggage. My mom says she'll have to work him over pretty hard for the next six months to do away with his whims, even though she claims that most of them are just due to him being so young and unruly."

We agreed to put Chareb into the paddock, letting him exercise himself for a while. While we led the ornery stallion between us over to the paddock, I heard a car turn into the farmyard. I turned my head, and stopped dead in my tracks. My heart must have skipped a beat, and I felt as if I had been hit in the stomach.

"Rachel!" I said, "That car that came into the farmyard, isn't that..."

Rachel nodded. She had a dark look on her face. "It looks exactly like the car that tried to run us down. But what is it doing here?"

The distance was too long to get a good look at the person behind the wheel. The car didn't stick around for long either. When the driver understood that we had seen the car, he started it fast and made it spin out into the road again, tires shrieking.

"It couldn't have been the same car!" I said when we had closed the gate to the paddock after putting Chareb in there. "They're all in jail, aren't they?"

"I'm sure it was the same car." Rachel's voice was insistent. "Maybe they lent it to a friend."

"But if so, what was he doing here?"

"Maybe he was just lost?" It didn't sound like Rachel believed her own suggestion.

"Or maybe... maybe it was the same person who threw the rock through the kitchen window?" I looked at Rachel.

"But why would he do that?" Rachel shook her head. "If it was one of the five Panthers, he... wait a minute. I want to check something."

Before I could open my mouth, she had run off in the direction of the house. I followed her slowly, while my thoughts were ransacking my brain. Vandalism in the night... a mysterious note... a car that just disappeared again... what the heck was going on?

122

I found out as soon as Rachel came back out. She looked livid. "I don't believe it!" she hissed. "I serve the police a gang of dangerous burglars and hoodlums on a silver platter, and they just let them go!"

"What do you mean? They're not in jail?" I stared at her in outrage.

"Nope, they got out already, yesterday afternoon. They had no grounds to hold them , according to the police officer that they reluctantly let me talk to."

"But... but... what about the evidence? The name... I mean Bertil... I mean..."

My confusion was complete, and I didn't say any more. My mind was bombarded with thoughts in all directions. If the Panthers were freed yesterday, and they had found out who had reported them... yes, that's how it must be. That would explain the note that was taped to the brick too. "We know it was you..." They had figured out that we were behind the police's suspicion against them, and now they were planning their revenge. "This is only the beginning", the note had said. My heart beat so hard it hurt. I was scared. Regardless of what the police thought, I didn't doubt for a second that the Panthers were behind the burglaries and the assaults. And what they had done to Mr. Anderson proved that they didn't shy away from anything.

I told Rachel what I was thinking, and she agreed. "We have to call the police and tell them that the Panthers threw the brick," I said frantically. "Then they'll have to arrest them again."

Rachel looked glum as she shook her head. "Don't you think I tried already? As soon as I found out that the Panthers had been set free, I understood who had been here last night. I tried to tell the police, and I also told them about the car, that it had tried to run us down, and that it appeared here on the farm."

"They didn't believe you?"

"It didn't sound like it. The officer I talked to just gave me some empty talk that was supposed to calm me down. I got so mad I felt like throwing a brick at *him*! If I had, I guess I could have just called it a prank."

Despite my fear, I had to smile, because I could just see Rachel sneaking after some big, burly police officer with a brick in her hand.

"No, I'm just talking nonsense," she said quickly. "A brick would have been too brutal. But a sloppy wet and icy cold sponge, maybe..."

"Good idea," I agreed. "I think I've heard that a cold compress is supposed to clear the head. If he won't listen to logic, maybe that's what he needs."

Chapter 11

We didn't see Stephanie all day, even though she had said the day before that she would be here. Maybe she was sick? I wondered if I ought to call her, but decided I'd better not, in case they were having family problems again. She'll show up tomorrow, I told myself.

We didn't feel very confident, either one of us, when Rachel and I were going to bed that night. We had tried to pretend that nothing was wrong while we ate tacos and watched TV. It was a movie with Jim Carrey, called "Liar Liar", about a slick lawyer who was a compulsive liar. His son made a wish that his dad would have to tell the truth for one whole day, and the wish came true. The movie was really funny, but I had a hard time concentrating.

In the middle of an hysterical scene in the court room, where the lawyer was using every trick to get the proceedings postponed until the next day so that he would be able to lie again, Rachel nudged me and said, "Too bad that isn't possible in real life. If the Panthers had been forced to tell the truth every time they opened their mouths, we wouldn't have to sit here pretending we aren't worried."

I thought about it while lying in my bed later, not able to sleep. Never before had I noticed how many different sounds there were in the house. It seemed like I heard creaking and groaning and clicking from every corner. But I tried to reassure myself that as long as Boris didn't react, there was no danger. He was lying on a blanket out in the hall, like a guard dog. Not much of a guard dog, if truth be told, but at least he would bark if there were intruders in the house, that's for sure. And Rachel had her cell phone on her nightstand, in case we had to call for help.

This time I didn't even have time to fall asleep before they came. The sound of someone walking on the gravel told me there was somebody out in the farmyard. I sat bolt upright in bed, my heart pounding. Boris hadn't made a sound yet. Were they going to break a window again, I wondered? I braced myself for the bang I expected to come. But everything was quiet out there now. Had I been wrong?

No, there was a sound again, but not from the house. It was a door creaking further away. The stable! I jumped out of bed, threw on the clothes that were lying ready at the end of the bed and bolted out the door. Boris was standing at the top of the stairs looking downstairs into the darkness, his ears moving slightly. He was obviously listening for something. When he started barking fiercely, it happened so suddenly I almost had a heart attack. Then he ran down the stairs and headed toward the front door.

I tore open the door to Rachel's room. "Rachel, get..."

"Hush, I'm trying to call," said Rachel abruptly. "If we can get the police here fast, they might catch the Panthers in the act."

I heard Rachel's voice as I sneaked quietly down the stairs. Boris stood by the front door and sniffed the crack around the door, while he switched between whimpering and scratching with his front paws. I grabbed the doorknob uncertainly. Did I dare go out there alone? Then I heard agitated neighing from the stable and a lot of thumps and bangs. It sounded like things were being thrown against the walls in there. Boris was barking like crazy now.

"I'm coming," Rachel's voice called out behind me. "And so are the police, I hope."

We tore the door open and ran out, just in time to see a person in black clothes bolting out the stable door. Before we could get a better look at the man; I only assumed it was a man, he disappeared around the corner of the stable and was gone.

Boris flew past us like a black and white shadow, while barking with everything he had. A second later he was also gone around the stable, chasing after the man.

Rachel and I rushed into the stable. I could feel the fear like a lump of ice in my stomach. Had he hurt the horses? The uproar of neighing in there could mean a lot of things.

"If he's done anything to the horses, I'll... I'll..." At that moment I couldn't even think of a bad enough punishment for such an atrocity. Fortunately the horses were only frightened, and not harmed.

The stable, on the other hand, looked like a tornado had whisked through it. Tools were scattered all over in a big jumble.

"Look at this," said Rachel as she pointed.

I looked into Chareb's stall, where a pitchfork was lying on the floor, with its sharp teeth facing upward. I felt myself getting hot with rage. If Chareb had stepped on the fork, or even worse, lain down on it, he could have been seriously injured.

I quickly removed the fork. I didn't care if it was evidence, I wasn't going to leave it in there with that wild thing of a horse a second longer I then searched the other stalls, but with the exception of a couple of grooming brushes in Baggi's stall, we didn't find anything suspicious.

I was just going into Quatana's stall when we heard Boris's barking turn into a heart-wrenching squeal. A moment later he came limping into the stable, with his tail between his legs. Clearly someone had kicked him really hard, but fortunately he didn't seem to be badly injured.

When the police came, there were no signs of the intruder. They dutifully searched the stable and area around it, and listened to what we told them. But it didn't look like they found any clues. Of course we told them again of our suspicion against the Panthers, but I had a sinking feeling that they didn't really take us seriously this time either. One of the police officers started talking about how easy it is to get deluded, and a bunch of blah, blah, blah about how our imagination can play tricks on us.

"What exactly are they imagining?" I said angrily after they were gone, "that the horses sneaked out of their stalls and started throwing tools around themselves?"

Rachel gave a slanted smile. "I think they're suspecting that we're overly nervous because of the incident with the brick last night, and that we were spooked and scared by nothing. They probably also think we may not have cleaned the stable properly last night. What do they know about horses or horse care? They might think we're not always that careful about tools lying around on the floor."

"Are you saying they actually think we made this mess ourselves?" I looked at Rachel in disbelief.

She shrugged her shoulders. "It kind of seemed that way."

"But what about the man, the person who came out from the stable? Do they think we imagined him too?"

Rachel shrugged her shoulders again. "Who knows what they think?" She yawned really big. "And right now I don't care what they believe. I'm so tired I can't think. Come on; let's go to bed. I'm sure the Panthers won't come back again tonight."

"No, but maybe tomorrow night," I said miserably. "What are we going to do, Rachel?"

"Sleep," said Rachel firmly. "Tomorrow we'll come up with a plan of action. No way am I going to let that gang continue to terrorize us! If the police won't help us, we'll just have to take care of it ourselves!"

Chapter 12

"Do you really think this will work?"

Rachel and I sat in our sleeping bags behind the tight row of bushes next to the garage. We could see both the stable and the house from here. But if Rachel was right, they would be vandalizing the car this time.

"I don't think they'll risk approaching the house or the stable this time," she had said when we discussed our plan earlier in the day. "But the garage is more hidden away, so they might count on not being discovered as easily there."

That is, if they're not planning to break into the house and attack us, I thought to myself. If so, it would be a good thing we weren't in the house, but were hiding outside.

"What if they don't come until the middle of the night, when it's pitch black?" I objected. "Then we won't get much use of that." I nodded toward the camera that was lying on the ground next to Rachel, ready for use.

"Let's just hope they come while there's still some light," said Rachel. "I would think they'd benefit from being able to see what they're doing too."

We sat in silence for a while. I felt my eyelids starting to get heavy. We hadn't exactly been getting much sleep lately, and we had a lot of work to do with the horses every day. Stephanie had stopped by briefly in the morning, but she had to go somewhere with her mom, and wasn't able to help out in the stable.

"But I'll be here first thing tomorrow morning," she said, "for sure."

I'd tried to ask her how things were going at home, but she just mumbled something evasive and left. Poor Stephanie, her life sure wasn't easy at the moment, I thought, yawning. Definitely not easy... and no wonder, because she was standing in the middle of the paddock trying to lead Chareb, but it didn't go very well. He was getting taller and taller with every circle he did, and finally Stephanie was lifted into the air by the long rope and flew away like a bird with Chareb going after her. They flew off toward the moon, and...

"Eva, wake up!" Rachel spoke urgently into my ear.

I looked around in confusion. I couldn't believe I had actually dozed off while sitting out here in the bushes. Incredible. I must be more tired than I was aware.

"Somebody's coming."

I didn't move a muscle as we listened to the sound of a car coming closer. Then suddenly the sound was gone.

"They probably didn't dare drive all the way up to the house, in case we heard them," whispered Rachel.

It was quiet again. Then we heard footsteps approaching, and voices mumbling quietly. I felt fear creeping up inside me. What if they discovered us sitting out here? What would they do then? Beat us to a pulp? Or worse?

But fortunately the footsteps stopped before they came close to us. It looked like Rachel was going to be right, they were heading for the car. To prevent the garage door from being destroyed, I had unlocked it earlier in the evening. I heard somebody grab the door handle, and then a triumphant laughter when they discovered that it was unlocked. A moment later all five had disappeared into the garage. Rachel crept forward in the bushes with the camera ready. But would the pictures be useful at all in this light? It had started getting dark, and inside the garage it was even darker.

I strained my eyes to see better. What were they doing in there? Oh-my-God! One of them had a huge knife, which he stabbed straight into one of the tires of the car. I felt Rachel tugging at my sleeve. "It's too dark," she hissed into my ear. "I can't take pictures without a flash, and if I use a flash, they'll see us. What do we do now?"

That's when I got my wild idea. If I had stopped to think about it, I would never have risked it. But I didn't think, because I was so angry... angry that there wouldn't be any photos, and angry because a gang of vicious bullies was standing there unperturbed in our garage, destroying our car. I waved the garage key in front of Rachel's eyes. She hesitated for a moment, then gave me a thumbs up signal.

We waited until all of them had their backs to the door. Then we ran as quietly as we could over to one side each of the doorway, grabbed the garage door and pulled with full force. I knew that my dad had recently oiled the hinges, but I was still not prepared for it to come down quite so fast. I just barely missed getting my foot caught as the door crashed against the ground.

"What the ..." came the roar from inside the garage.

"The key! Hurry!" screamed Rachel and held down the door handle with all her might.

I pushed the key into the lock and turned it. My hands trembled so much I couldn't believe I made it. And not just my hands, my entire body trembled like pudding in an earthquake.

"That's what I call a fine catch," said Rachel triumphantly as she pulled out the cell phone. She ignored the ugly shouting and cursing that came from inside the garage.

"Hello, I need the police. We have a small problem here, or rather five..."

Chapter 13

"I will never forget the looks on their faces when the five of them came out of the garage and walked right into the arms of the police officers," laughed Rachel. "What a great moment!"

I laughed. That was my favorite part as well. "They couldn't talk themselves out of this one, at least. I hope they'll get locked up for a long time."

"I think they will," said Rachel. "This time the police will push them a little harder, so hopefully they'll end up admitting the burglaries too."

But that's not what happened, because something else occurred which completely clashed with our theory of the Panthers being the burglars. That night, while the Panthers were in police custody, an elderly man got burglarized in his own home while he was sleeping. And the thieves left the usual "signature."

Rachel and I were completely baffled. We had been so sure that the Panthers were guilty, but evidently that wasn't the case after all. The symbol couldn't be an imitation, either, because the police had never revealed what it looked like. I knew it, of course, because I had seen it in Mr. Anderson's house, but there couldn't be too many people who knew what it looked like, at least not well enough to imitate it.

We discussed the problem while we were doing the morning chores in the stable, but without getting anywhere. Finally we gave up and started planning a fun horseback ride instead.

Quatana was being really cuddly this morning. She rubbed her head against my arm, pushed her muzzle against my pockets in search of treats, and was generally in the way while I was trying to work. But I couldn't get mad at her, because she's so adorable when she's in that mood. I find her irresistible. I took a break from the grooming and just scratched her and cuddled her for a while. She loved it. Her eyelids started drooping and she made some funny little noises in her throat, the way she does when she thinks life is very, very good.

Stephanie wasn't there yet, as she had promised. I figured she would show up any time but her mom came instead.

"I'm sorry to disturb you," she said and hastily backed away from Baggi's curious muzzle. He wanted to check out the new visitor, but she was obviously not used to horses.

"Is something wrong?" I asked. "Is Stephanie sick?"

Stephanie's mom shook her head. "No, she's perfectly fine, even if she's had a rough time lately. Which I'm sure you know?"

She looked questioningly at me, and I nodded.

"Stephanie asked me to tell you that she'll be here this afternoon. She promised to go with Robert into the city this morning and take care of something."

"Who's Robert?" Rachel asked curiously.

"Robert is Stephanie's brother. "I guess you wouldn't know his name, since he refuses to use it. Childish, isn't it? He insists on being called Rob. Refuses to answer if I use his real name. Even his teachers call him Rob."

When Stephanie's mom was gone, Rachel and I looked at each other over Baggi's back. Baggi chowed down on some fresh, savory hay and didn't pay any attention to us. We probably looked equally silly, both of us.

"Robert!" said Rachel, "Bert! Is it really possible that..."

I cut her off. "That explains everything!" I said eagerly. "No wonder Stephanie has looked so downhearted and strange lately. I bet you she suspects her brother. She must have understood all along that "Bert" could have been an attempt at saying "Robert." Do you remember how relieved she looked when it seemed like the Panthers were the guilty ones?"

"And she didn't say a word, even when it looked like Mr. Anderson would die!" Rachel threw her arm out angrily and accidentally hit Baggi in the neck. He jumped in surprise and looked at her resentfully. What kind of nonsense was this? Can't a good horse stand here and eat in peace anymore?

Rachel scratched his mane apologetically. "I'm sorry, Baggi. I'm not mad at you. You just go on eating."

Baggi flapped his ears and lowered his head as he resumed eating his hay.

When we were all done in the stable, Rachel and I went for a ride. I tried to relax and enjoy myself while sitting on Quatana's back, but my mind was so chock full of confused thoughts that I barely registered where we were going. It looked like Rachel felt the same way. The problem was that we felt so helpless. What could we do? It was one thing to suspect Rob of being the brutal burglar and attacker, but proving it was an entirely different matter. I had suggested that we call the police, but Rachel didn't think that was such a good idea.

"We don't have the slightest bit of evidence," she said, and I reluctantly had to admit she was right.

We had been so sure that we knew who it was once before, so why would the police think we knew this time? Sure, we'd been right about it being the Panthers who were terrorizing us. But that was apparently an act of revenge for having gotten them in trouble with the police for no reason whatsoever.

When we came back from our ride, Stephanie was sitting outside waiting for us. She had let Boris out of his "prison cell" in the stable, and was scratching his soft fur. Boris looked like he was in heaven. This was much better than being locked up in that stupid stall in the stable.

Rachel and I had decided not to let on that we knew anything to Stephanie, but it wasn't easy. Fortunately she wasn't in a very talkative mood. She seemed distant and preoccupied while we walked around the pastures, checking on the horses that were being kept outside. I couldn't get enough of the little foals out there, tagging along with their mothers. Some of them were lying down, sleeping in the grass. Others were jumping around, all excited and happy to be alive. They were incredibly cute and I got warm inside by watching them.

We had put a leash on Boris, and he seemed a little offended that he didn't get to run into the pastures and play with the horses. He was tugging on the leash and tilting his head in a begging sort of way, as if to say, "Couldn't I just play with one single horse for a little bit? Please? It's been so long since I got to do that."

But he was stuck with the leash until we got back to the farm-yard.

The whole time we were inspecting the pastures, we walked around thinking about Rob and what he had done. Back at the stable, while Stephanie was upstairs in the hayloft on an errand, I pulled Rachel aside into Quatana's stall.

"I've been thinking," I said quickly.

"Congratulations! How does it feel?"

"Oh, cut it out, I'm being serious. We just have to report our suspicions about Rob to the police."

"But we don't have..." started Rachel.

"... the slightest bit of evidence," I finished. "I know. And maybe the police will just brush off what we say. But I know one thing; if we don't report it, and there is a new burglary and some-one gets hurt, I won't be able to sleep another night for the rest of my life. I would feel it was my fault for not doing anything to prevent it."

"I see what you mean," said Rachel, "but I... oh no, I don't think we should increase Quatana's oat ration. She looks just fine to me."

I was about to open my mouth and ask what the heck she was talking about, when I realized that Stephanie was standing in the hallway. Had she heard us? I thought her face looked a little funny. But no, it didn't sound like it; she just wanted to ask if she should get some hay for Chareb, or if he was going outside tonight.

135

"I think we'll put him in the stable," I said.

"Ok, then I'll fill his hay net," said Stephanie as she left.

Rachel and I didn't dare to say any more about the burglaries as long as Stephanie was there. We talked about the horses instead, and after a while the conversation turned, for some reason, to movies.

"I saw in the newspaper that there's a good movie out right now," said Rachel. "I think it's got horses in it, and it's received good reviews."

"Sounds good," I said excitedly. "Do you want to go and see it some night? There's not much good on TV anyway, and a film about horses has to be okay!"

"It'll have to be tonight, then," said Rachel, "because tonight's its last night at the local movie theater."

"Great," I said. "Would you like to go, Stephanie?"

Stephanie nodded. "Sure," she said. "Sounds like fun."

We agreed to meet at 7:45 p.m. outside the movie theater. Then Stephanie went home, and Rachel and I went inside to eat.

Chapter 14

"Honestly, this is getting to be a bit too late," said Rachel and looked at her watch for about the tenth time. "We agreed on 7:45, and it's almost eight. The movie is starting in a couple of minutes. I don't think Stephanie is coming. But what are we going to do with her ticket?"

Rachel had bought tickets for all three of us when she and I got to the theater at the agreed time.

"Look who's coming," I said and nudged Rachel.

Rob was running down the street as if he had a police mob after him. Maybe he knew where Stephanie was? If he'd care to answer, that is.

But I didn't have to ask. To my surprise, Rob came straight over to Rachel and me. He was short of breath.

"Stephanie got sick," he said. "I was supposed to tell you that she's sorry. It's a stomach flu or something. She's home throwing up."

I flinched. Poor Stephanie.

"Thanks for letting us know," said Rachel. "We'd better get in there. The movie is starting. Too bad about her ticket, though. Do you want it?" She looked at Rob.

I expected him to sneer contemptuously. A horse film was hardly up his alley, but he just said: "Why not? I don't have anything else to do right now anyway."

We just made it in time for the movie. Rob plopped into the seat next to me. He didn't say a word throughout the entire movie, which, by the way, was excellent, but also very sad. A beautiful horse died because someone drugged it. They didn't intend for it to die; they just wanted to prevent it from running a race in which

137

it was the favorite. Fortunately the bandits were caught in the end, just as they were going to do the same to the horse that had the star role in the movie. It was so suspenseful I could hardly sit still.

Now and then I glanced over at Rob briefly. He had the same somber look on his face the whole time. It didn't seem like the action made any impression on him. Even during the saddest parts, where I was fighting back tears, which made it hard to see the screen, he just sat there seemingly unperturbed. Maybe he didn't have any feelings? If he was the callous criminal we suspected him to be, he had to be pretty heartless. Someone who assaults elderly people with no concern for the consequences probably doesn't get stirred up when a horse or two dies.

When we got up to leave after the show, I saw that Rob wasn't the only one who seemed out of place in the movie theater. A few rows in front of us were the five members of the Panthers gang. They were apparently not in police custody anymore. I felt my heart start beating fast from fear.

They must be even keener on revenge now that Rachel and I had fooled them so thoroughly.

I made Rachel aware of them, and we waited to leave the theater until almost everyone else had gone. Rob didn't even say bye; he just disappeared without saying a word.

Outside in the street my eyes searched for the Panthers. Fortunately I didn't see them anywhere.

"What if they're standing in an alleyway, waiting for us to pass?" I said nervously.

"Take it easy," said Rachel. "I don't think they saw us at all."

I still didn't feel safe until we passed Burger King. We could see a long line in there. People were obviously hungry after the movie. I saw the Panthers in the line too, all five of them. Seeing them in there made me relax. Rob was there too. He was standing at the end of the line, staring gloomily at the floor.

Rachel and I hurried past the windows and headed home.

"Please tell me this is a bad dream!"

I was standing in the middle of the living room floor looking at the chaos around me. It looked exactly like it had in Mr. Anderson's house. Drawers and cabinets had been emptied, pillows and blankets were scattered around the floor. The only difference was that, fortunately, there was no unconscious man on the floor.

"The camera is gone," reported Rachel. "And the cell phone." Other than those two items, it didn't look like anything was missing. However it was hard to tell in such a chaotic mess. We saw signs that indicated the thief or thieves had looked in the kitchen cabinets, too, but fortunately they hadn't found the food money.

"My mom's jewelry!" I screamed, and stormed up the stairs to the second floor. However, up there everything seemed to be untouched. There was no sign that the intruders had gone upstairs at all. That's funny. Had they been interrupted?

"Where's Boris?" I said when I came back downstairs and we had called the police. Calling the police station was starting to feel like routine. By now we even knew the number by heart.

"I have no idea," said Rachel. "He was sleeping in the kitchen when we left. Most likely he managed to get outside and run away."

I felt myself get cold. What if the burglar had hurt Boris, or even worse? No I didn't even want to think about it.

"Look at this!" said Rachel. The living room door had been wide open when we walked in. Rachel had just pushed it shut with her foot. She didn't want to touch the door handle in case the burglar had left fingerprints on it. I just stood there gaping by surprise. Someone had sprayed a sign on the wall, which I had seen before and would never forget. Last time I saw that sign was on Mr. Anderson's wall - a kind of strange, curled snake.

But then...that meant...Rachel and I looked helplessly at each other. We couldn't find words.

Chapter 15

"I give up!" said Rachel, and threw the grooming brush aside with such force that it bounced across the stable floor. "I don't get it."

She looked at Boris who chased delightedly after the grooming brush. Apparently he thought this was some kind of new, exciting game. He ran back to Rachel triumphantly with the brush in his mouth, and tilted his head, as if to say, C'mon, throw it again!

I'd been so relieved when Boris showed up again the night before, because I had really been worried about him. But he seemed quite contented and unharmed.

"Some watchdog you are!" Rachel said and shook her head at him. "We get burglars breaking into the house, and what do you do? Disappear! I sure wish you could talk, so you could tell us who came over - was it several people, or just one person?"

Boris didn't have any answer for that. He just shook his fur and padded happily over to his water bowl.

We hadn't slept much that night, but I guess we were getting used to that by now. The police had come over, and after they had left again we sat up and talked until late into the night.

As it turned out, we were sure happy we hadn't gotten around to telling the police about our suspicion against Rob. That would have been a total embarrassment. Because this time Rob had a foolproof alibi. He had been sitting next to us in the movie theater, and when we went home, he had gone to Burger King. And no way would he have had enough time to do the burglary before the movie. That was out of the question. The Panthers gang had the same alibi, of course, as we had also seen them in the movie theater and in the line at Burger King afterwards.

"We're back at square one, except I understand less and less,"

140

sighed Rachel. "No, Boris, give me back that brush. We're not playing right now."

"Woof!" said Boris, grabbing the brush with his teeth and taking off like a bullet out of the stable.

"Let him go," I said. "He'll get tired soon enough. Here, take this brush instead."

I threw it over to her, and she set about grooming Baggi's flanks with resolute energy.

"I swear I'll never again brag about being a good detective," she went on. "Talk about being on the wrong track."

We were still harping on the same subject when Stephanie came by. She looked pretty pale, and no wonder, since she had just had the stomach flu.

"I feel a lot better now," she said.

We told her about the burglary, and she was shocked at the news. The burglars had gotten in through a basement window, which evidently had not been closed properly.

"It's not even possible to close it any better," I said. "It's probably been like that for a long time, without anyone noticing. Pretty funny, actually. Here we've been super diligent about locking up all the doors, while that window has been open all along. All that was missing was a door mat outside the window with a 'Welcome' message on it."

"We've called someone to come and fix the window, but the guy can't make it until the day after tomorrow," said Rachel. "But it doesn't really matter. It's probably not very likely that the thieves will come back."

Now that Rob was above suspicion, we also told her, with some embarrassment, what we had thought. Stephanie didn't say much to this, and I was thinking she probably had suspected the same thing herself.

Rachel suggested we go for a ride. At first Stephanie said yes, but then she suddenly wasn't so sure she felt up to it after all. I noticed she touched her throat several times, so I asked if she wasn't feeling well.

She shook her head. "I just got a little dizzy. It's probably because I haven't eaten for so long. I think I'd better go home. Have a nice ride. Will you be going right away?"

"As soon as we've saddled up the horses. We need a mega dose of fresh air after last night's shock," said Rachel.

Two hours later we were heading back home again. The ride hadn't been very long. Both Rachel and I were tired and unfocused. The horses noticed, of course, especially Baggi. He got grouchy and rebellious, constantly trying to turn back to go home. We made a halfhearted attempt at a galloping race across a field. That got Baggi going, and he really stretched out. But then Quatana got difficult. She threw her head to the side, dancing sideways, obviously not at all concerned that Rachel and Baggi had almost reached the finish line before we got started.

We decided to leave the horses in the paddock when we got home, and go and take a nap.

"What, is this place haunted, or has someone been here while we were gone?" Rachel scratched her head and looked around the living room. "I'm sure I had all the throw pillows piled up at the end of the couch, but now they're scattered around all over it.

"You must have forgotten something," I said, and yawned.

"But the chairs have been moved too. I remember specifically that I placed one of them much closer to the window than where it is now. And there's more. Eva, someone has been here while we were out, I'm quite sure!"

We looked at each other.

"The money!" screamed Rachel and bolted for the kitchen. "It's okay, it's still there," she said with relief when she came back.

"So the person who was here didn't steal anything," I said, surprised. "But what in the world was he doing then?"

"Looking for something, maybe?" Rachel wrinkled her forehead and thought hard. Something he lost during the burglary. Maybe he came back to find it.

"Do you think he did?"

Rachel shook her head. "If he had lost something in here, the police would have found it for sure, she said. "Remember they pretty much combed the entire living room searching for clues."

"Maybe he just thought he had lost something," I suggested with uncertainty.

"Or maybe he lost it somewhere else, like outside for instance." Rachel looked meaningfully at me. "Should we look around the outside of the house and see if we find anything interesting?"

"What about the basement, where the thief came in?" I asked. "By the way, he must have taken that route this time too, since there's no sign of a break-in."

"Let's take a look. Come on, what are we waiting for?"

We searched the yard and the flowerbeds near the basement window without finding anything. A search of the basement didn't turn up anything either. We were about to give up when Rachel suddenly yelled: "Eva, look at this!"

She was standing on the stairs pointing. A dusty beam of light streaked through one of the basement windows, just bright enough to make a shimmer on something small lying in a crack of the basement floor. Had it not been for that beam of light, we wouldn't have seen the little metallic sparkle.

"It must have dropped when the burglar went up the stairs," said Rachel excitedly as she carefully picked the small object out of the crack in the floor.

She held it up to the light so we could both see it properly. I stared at it, completely numb with disappointment. It was an old beer cap, which must have lain there for years.

Chapter 16

"Stand still, Quatana. How many times do I have to tell you to stop pretending you're ticklish?"

I waved the grooming brush threateningly in front of her nose, but it didn't make the slightest bit of impression on Quatana.

Rachel and I had tethered the horses out in the farmyard in the nice weather, so we could do the grooming out there. They were pretty dusty after playing in the paddock all afternoon.

The disappointment after our unsuccessful search expedition was still lingering inside me. I felt kind of like I was standing outside myself, watching as I groomed Quatana.

A voice suddenly broke through my clouded mind, startling me so much I almost dropped the brush. I turned around, rather relieved by the interruption.

"Hi, Stephanie," I said. "It's nice of you to come. I hadn't really expected to see you anymore today."

She still didn't look quite well, I thought, but she insisted that she was completely fine again, so I had to believe her.

"Should I groom Primanka?" she asked. "I feel bad that I haven't helped out very much lately."

"Don't," I said. "It's not your fault you got sick, or that you've been having problems with your brother."

"If you only knew..." she started saying, but stopped. "Gosh, here I go, just chatting instead of working. I'll go and get Primanka. Is she in the big pasture?"

I nodded, and looked after her as she rushed off. She'd been about to tell me something. I wondered what it was.

When she came back with Primanka by her side, Rachel and I

144

had started speculating about the burglary again. Stephanie joined in.

"It seems really mysterious," she said. "Especially with that snake that was sprayed on the wall. Do you think the police will ever figure it out?"

"I have no idea," I said honestly. "It doesn't look very promising. What do you think, Rachel?"

There was no answer. Rachel just stood there, with a funny expression on her face. It almost looked like she didn't know where she was.

"Earth to Rachel!" I said teasingly. "What's the matter? Have you fallen asleep on your feet with your eyes wide open?"

Rachel started. Then she shook her head and forced a smile. "I'm sorry, I guess I was off in my own world," she said.

I looked at her searchingly. Rachel saw the look in my eyes, and laughed.

"I'm back," she said. "What were you saying?"

"Oh, I don't remember," I said and started laughing too.

Rachel seemed pretty distracted for the rest of the afternoon. I wondered what she was thinking about.

When Stephanie had gone home that evening, and Rachel and I were making dinner, she finally told me. Rachel said with a sly smile, "Would you like to catch a burglar, Eva?"

"You bet," I said excitedly. "Are you saying you have an idea?"

Rachel nodded. "More than an idea, in fact. I'm sure I've got it now. It was something Stephanie said that made me think."

I couldn't remember Stephanie saying anything particularly interesting, and started feeling rather dumb.

But when Rachel told me her thoughts, I finally saw the light. "Of course," I said. "That's it! But how on earth are we going to prove it?"

"By placing some bait," said Rachel with a big grin on her face. "Now listen, here's what we'll do. First, you have to make a call. It's more natural if you're the one calling. Then..."

Chapter 17

"How long are we going to sit here in the dark?" I whispered grumpily to Rachel.

It was almost one o'clock in the morning, and I was so tired I was seeing double. "If nobody comes, then we'll have wasted another night's sleep."

"I'm quite sure somebody will come. You said exactly what I told you to say, right?"

"Yes, I did. The whole bit. Even your ridiculous idea of having put what we found in the fridge, because no one would think to look there."

Rachel had cooked up a story about how we'd found something that the burglar had lost while he was in the house. This object was something that the police could use to track down the burglar. We were going to give it to the police tomorrow, and in the meantime we had hidden it in the fridge.

"But how do you know that the burglar didn't find what he was after when he came back to search?" I had argued when Rachel had told me the story I was supposed to relay over the phone.

"If it's what I think it is, the thing is still missing," Rachel had said, in her irritatingly mysterious way. "You ought to know what it is too. I say, kids today are not very observant."

I threatened to strangle her if she didn't tell me what it was. When she finally did, I knew she was right. I was not very observant.

I was just about to doze off when I suddenly heard something. Somebody was opening the basement window! In a flash I was wide awake.

"Rachel," I whispered. "Did you hear that?"

"See, what did I tell you?" mumbled Rachel. "Now we'll just have to wait."

There was a creak on the stairs. Then we heard stealthy footsteps across the hall, followed by the quiet click of a door being opened. Whoever was in there was going into the kitchen.

Rachel and I sneaked over to the kitchen door as quietly as we could. Then Rachel tore the door open. I turned on the light, and we stared at the two who had just opened the door to the fridge.

Rob and Stephanie stared back at us, frozen to the spot.

"Hi there!" said Rachel cheerfully. "Looking for a late night snack? Is your own fridge empty?"

"We can explain..." Stephanie stopped. I'm sure she understood that there were no explanations that could get them out of this situation.

"Or maybe you were you looking for your necklace?" Rachel continued.

Stephanie's hand made an involuntary motion toward her neck.

"Sorry, then, I'll have to disappoint you. It's not here. That was just a trick to get you here. We weren't even certain that it was your necklace that you were looking for when you came back and rummaged through the house this morning. We only guessed. You know, you always used to wear it, and then it was suddenly gone."

"But how did you know..."

"That it was you, you mean? Well, you gave yourself away earlier today, when you mentioned the snake symbol. Eva and I hadn't told you that the symbol was a snake, so how did you know that? After that I put two and two together, and decided to make a trap to see if it really was you. Having Rob walk into the trap with you is definitely an extra bonus!"

Chapter 18

"I'm so glad it's over." Rachel tossed her riding helmet aside and shook her long, blond hair.

It was the day after we exposed Stephanie and Rob. We were riding in the woods and had stopped for a while in a clearing. Quatana and Baggi were tethered to a tree, and Rachel and I had sat down on the grass to rest for a while.

"I had to pinch myself to be sure it wasn't a dream," I said. "Now the whole thing seems unreal." I thought back to the events of last night, and Rob's pitiful attempt at getting away.

"We haven't actually done anything wrong," he tried. "It was a stupid thing to do, but we were only..." Rob looked at the floor, as if hoping to find inspiration there.

"You might as well tell us the truth," said Rachel. "Because we know the whole story. Besides, we just found out at the hospital today that Mr. Anderson is awake, and then it won't be long before he can tell everything to the police."

Rachel was bluffing again. It was true that Mr. Anderson was awake, but the problem was that he didn't remember anything at all from the assault. But Rob didn't know that. And he broke like a bubble.

"But it wasn't me who struck him! It wasn't me! It was Berry. He was bragging about it afterwards. I started to keep watch for them sometimes while they were doing a burglary, but then they started hurting people. I tried to quit then, but they threatened me..."

Rob dropped down on a kitchen chair and put his head in his

148

hands. He looked completely beat. Stephanie started crying. I felt sorry for her.

We gradually got the whole story. How Rob had started hanging around the Panthers because he didn't have any friends. In the beginning he thought it was just exciting and cool. He stole cigarettes and other stuff for them in the stores. He was too naive to understand that the Panthers were just using him. They managed to get him in on the burglaries as well. He would be their lookout and let them know if anyone was coming.

But when they started using violence against people, he got scared. He didn't want to be part of that. That's when he found out that it wasn't as simple to break with the Panthers. They threatened his life, and what was worse, they threatened to hurt Stephanie. It got so bad that he went into hiding for a while, in a house that he knew was empty because the owners were on vacation. He was very relieved when he heard that they'd been arrested, but they managed to get a message to him. Commit a burglary and sign with the snake symbol, or else...

Rob didn't dare disobey, so the Panthers were let go, and the nightmare and pressure continued. The thought of Stephanie and his parents finding out what he had done kept him from going to the police with his story.

Stephanie had long understood that something was seriously wrong with Rob, because of his moodiness and strange behavior. When she overheard Rachel and me suspecting him of being behind the burglary and the assaults, she had confronted him.

Rob broke down and told her everything. Then he begged her to help him with an alibi. She had refused at first, but eventually she had agreed to do it. She couldn't stand the thought of her twin brother getting into serious trouble with the police.

"My dad went to jail for major fraud," she sniffled. "How would my mom feel if Rob also ended up in jail?"

"Maybe Rob should have thought about that before he got involved with a gang like that," said Rachel in a hard voice. "Besides, I think Rob is probably too young to go to jail."

Stephanie sniffled. "Anyway, we agreed on a plan. I would pretend to be sick last night, and then Rob would show up outside the movie theater at the last minute and go with you. The thought of breaking into your house made me sick, Eva, so I was really happy to find that open basement window. I rummaged around a bit, but made sure not to break anything. Then I sprayed the snake symbol on the wall, the way Rob had showed me, grabbed the camera and the cell phone, and got out of there as fast as I could. Both items are hidden in a safe place, because I wanted to return them anonymously later."

Then Stephanie discovered that she had lost her necklace. She was scared to death, and came back to look for it while Rachel and I went for a ride. But she hadn't found it. Naturally she took the bait when I called and told her that we had found a piece of evidence which we were going to give to the police, and so she and Rob came to get it, and by doing so, gave themselves away.

"Are you sleeping, Eva?"

I started. I had been so deep in thought that I hadn't heard Rachel talking to me.

"Of course not," I said. "I was just thinking about everything that happened. What were you saying?"

"That it was 'nice' of Rob to provide an extra alibi for the Panthers while he was getting one for himself," she said with sarcasm. "The worst part is that he actually claimed that it was a coincidence that they were also at that movie, and that he hadn't told them."

"You don't believe him?"

Rachel shook her head. "Nope," she said firmly. "I think Rob told them so they could make sure that we saw them. It didn't look like they noticed us, but I'd be willing to bet that they did. I think they made sure we had seen them before they left the movie theater."

"Be that as it may," I said as I stretched. "Now that the police know the truth, they can take care of the rest, along with his parents."

We had called their mom and stepdad first on the night before, because Stephanie had asked us to. After they came, their mother had called the police herself. Her face had been one stiff mask and she had moved around like a robot. I assumed it was the shock. I felt terribly sorry for her.

"I guess we won't see Stephanie around the stable anymore," Rachel said as we rode home a little while later. But she was wrong. When we rode into the farmyard, we saw Stephanie sitting on the gravel by the stable door, with her head down. Next to her was a little sports bag.

She didn't look up until we had stepped down from the saddles. Then she lifted her head and glanced timidly up at us.

"Hi," said Rachel in a neutral voice. "You're an unexpected guest, I must say."

Stephanie tried to say something, but only uttered a choked sort of sound. She cleared her throat and tried again.

"I'll leave right away," she said. "I just wanted to say how really sorry I am about everything. I really made a mess of things. If I had only given it more thought..."

She shook her head and hid her face in her hands.

Rachel tethered Baggi to the stable wall and went over to her. I stood where I was, drawn between anger and pity. What exactly did she expect? That we would give her a hug and happily proclaim that everything was forgiven?

"I know you can't forgive me," continued Stephanie and looked up, as if she had read my mind. "You don't have to tell me that I behaved like an idiot, because I know. And if I hadn't understood that much by myself, I certainly got to hear it over the last few hours first from the police, and then from my mom and Steve. I think I've had enough scolding to last me a life time."

Well deserved! I thought, trying to hold on to my anger. That wasn't easy, because Stephanie was a pitiful sight sitting there. Rachel had sat down next to her, without saying anything.

"I know you don't want to see me right now, but I didn't want to be so cowardly that I didn't at least try to put some things right again." She opened the sports bag and pulled out the camera and the cell phone. "Here you go, she said and held both items out to me. "They're both fine."

When I didn't make any move to take them, she gave them to Rachel. Then she got up, brushed off the back of her pants and said quietly: "Well, I'll go now. It was great being able to come here to the stable. I'll miss it."

"So what will happen now?" asked Rachel. "I mean, with you and Rob."

"I don't know," said Stephanie, and shrugged her shoulders with a sigh. "Rob may be sent away somewhere. My mom is going to talk to the Children's Services about it. I may be let off with the scolding I've already gotten..." She shrugged again and put her bag over her shoulder. "...and with losing the only friends I had around here." The last statement was uttered so quietly that I could barely hear it.

She walked toward the road without looking back. I felt a knot in my stomach. Rachel looked at me. There was a hint of blame in her eyes, I thought. But what did she expect me to do? Forgive Stephanie, just like that? That was out of the question.

Why not, asked a voice inside me. What, do you think you're so perfect? What Stephanie did, she did for her brother. It was stupid, but what do you know about having a sibling? Maybe you would have done the same if you had a brother who was in trouble.

Something loosened up inside me. What was I thinking? Did I really want to give up a good horse friend, who had always been there for me when I needed her, just because she made a mistake? A big mistake, but still... She certainly had to pay for it, and it wouldn't be easy for her if they sent Rob away. Was I really that heartless? No, I wasn't.

"Stephanie!" I called. "Wait! Don't go!"

I ran after her as fast as I could.

152

Epilogue

"I can't believe it's only a week until school starts again. Where did the summer go?" Stephanie stroked her hair back from her forehead and grabbed a tail brush.

"Well you know what they say, time flies when you're having fun," I said. "Apparently it's true."

"Yes, we have certainly had some fun," said Stephanie as she patted Primanka's flank. "At least these last weeks."

A shadow seemed to cross her face, and I knew she was thinking about the difficult days earlier in the summer, when everything seemed hopeless.

"Have you heard anything from Rob lately?" I asked.

"Yeah, he called yesterday. He seems really happy. He and Grandpa had been out fishing all day, and Rob was bragging about a big fish he caught. It got bigger and bigger during our conversation." Stephanie laughed.

"Do you miss him?" I asked slowly.

"I miss the brother I had before he changed and tried to be so cool and all," said Stephanie. She was pulling a handful of straw out of Primanka's tail and started brushing it carefully. "But I think it was good for everybody that he got to move in with Grandma and Grandpa for a year and go to school there. Rob has always gotten along really well with Grandpa."

"By the way, I was supposed to say hi from Rachel," I said. "She called last night and said she'll be coming over for a visit this weekend."

"Great!" said Stephanie "Then we can all go for a ride together!"

"Sure we will," I said, "and we can…"

I didn't finish, because just then Nabila, one of our breeding

153

mares, came across the farmyard with her foal in tow. How in the world did she get out of the enclosure where she normally stayed? I must not have closed the gate properly.

"Hey, stop!" I yelled and chased after the runaway, who seemed to have no intention of obeying. We'd better enjoy our freedom while we have it, seemed to be Nabila's thoughts.

I suddenly heard the sound of excited barking. Boris! Mr. Anderson was long since back from the hospital, and had recovered completely from the assault, so Boris had moved back home. But he came over to visit every single day, and I liked that. Right now, however, was definitely not a good time. A runaway horse and a dog that loved to tease horses was a bad combination, I thought. Besides, Nabila was a very protective mother, and she probably wouldn't accept any intrusion from a yapping dog.

Wild with excitement, Boris shot over toward Nabila, barking up a storm. Nabila was taken by surprise and stopped, seemingly uncertain how she should handle this pushy little fur ball that was jumping back and forth in front of her and the foal. The foal got closer to its mom, while staring at Boris with big, bewildered eyes. Boris's ears were flapping in pure excitement, and for a moment they looked more like a pair of butterfly wings.

I took advantage of the confusion and managed to grab the runaway. Nabila stomped her legs, but stopped fairly quickly and allowed me to lead her back to the pasture without further ado. The foal followed us closely while keeping a watchful eye on Boris. He had stopped barking and looked completely innocent.

I looked at him and he wagged his tail happily. That was fun!

"You're the biggest rascal there is, you know that?" I said. "But for once you were actually kind of useful, so I'll forgive you this time.

I looked sternly at him. "But you're going to have to stop fooling around with the horses, do you hear?"

Boris wagged his tail agreeably. But he had a look in his eyes that made me think it was hardly the last time he would cause a commotion around the horses. I'm sure Stephanie and I had a few more surprises ahead of us before the summer was over.